Seven Paths
to Death

Seven Paths
to Death

A SAMURAI MYSTERY

DOROTHY
&
THOMAS
HOOBLER

PHILOMEL BOOKS

PHILOMEL BOOKS
A division of Penguin Young Readers Group.
Published by The Penguin Group.
Penguin Group (USA) Inc., 375 Hudson Street, New York, NY 10014, U.S.A.
Penguin Group (Canada), 90 Eglinton Avenue East, Suite 700, Toronto, Ontario M4P 2Y3, Canada
(a division of Pearson Penguin Canada Inc.).
Penguin Books Ltd, 80 Strand, London WC2R 0RL, England.
Penguin Ireland, 25 St. Stephen's Green, Dublin 2, Ireland (a division of Penguin Books Ltd).
Penguin Group (Australia), 250 Camberwell Road, Camberwell, Victoria 3124, Australia
(a division of Pearson Australia Group Pty Ltd).
Penguin Books India Pvt Ltd, 11 Community Centre, Panchsheel Park, New Delhi - 110 017, India.
Penguin Group (NZ), 67 Apollo Drive, Rosedale, North Shore 0632, New Zealand
(a division of Pearson New Zealand Ltd).
Penguin Books (South Africa) (Pty) Ltd, 24 Sturdee Avenue, Rosebank, Johannesburg 2196, South Africa.
Penguin Books Ltd, Registered Offices: 80 Strand, London WC2R 0RL, England.

Copyright © 2008 by Dorothy and Thomas Hoobler

Published simultaneously in Canada. Printed in the United States of America.
Design by Katrina Damkoehler. Text set in New Baskerville.

Library of Congress Cataloging-in-Publication Data
Hoobler, Dorothy.
Seven paths to death : a samurai mystery / Dorothy and Thomas Hoobler.   p. cm.
Summary: Samurai Seikei and Judge Ooka, his foster-father, seek seven men who have seven maps on their
backs in order to locate a cache of dangerous weapons before they fall into the wrong hands.
1. Japan—History—Tokugawa period, 1600–1868—Juvenile fiction. [1. Japan—History—Tokugawa period,
1600–1868—Fiction. 2. Samurai—Fiction. 3. Maps—Fiction. 4. Weapons—Fiction. 5. Tattooing—Fiction.
6. Mystery and detective stories.] I. Hoobler, Thomas. II. Title.
PZ7.H76227Sev 2008   [Fic]—dc22   2007042092

ISBN 978-0-399-24610-4
1 3 5 7 9 10 8 6 4 2

To our agent, Al Zuckerman,
who has always believed in our work.

CONTENTS

Seven Paths
to Death

PROLOGUE

It was supposed to be a joyous day. Each spring the villagers awakened the Ta No Kami, the spirit of the rice, with dancing and song. The rapid booming of drums announced the appearance of Amaterasu, the sun goddess. When her beams shone across the dark waters of the rice paddies, the young girls of the village raised their voices in welcome. Their older sisters began to dance across the wooden platforms that crisscrossed the shallow water. Another group of young people waited for a signal from the village chief. The rice seedlings that they held would then be transplanted into the paddies, marking the beginning of this year's crop.

The kami of the rice, who had been asleep all winter, now would awaken to these pleasant sounds. In a benevolent mood, he would repay the villagers with a plentiful harvest. A quantity of the very best rice from last year had been saved and would be cooked and eaten at today's feast, which all would share.

No one had ever actually seen the rice spirit, but neither did anyone doubt his existence. For clearly it was a great and powerful

force that visited the rice paddies, causing the plants to grow and bringing prosperity—and life itself—to the village year after year.

But this year, as the ceremony was reaching its height, someone saw a ripple in the water, some distance from where the seedlings were about to be planted. A boy pointed to the spot and cried out, but his mother hushed him. Someone else noticed, but thought it was only a carp that had somehow gotten into the paddy.

Then it emerged from the water, and everyone saw. The music slowed, then stopped, and the dancers froze. A village elder with poor eyesight motioned furiously for them to begin again, thinking that this must be a visible manifestation of Ta No Kami. An unparalleled honor for the village. When the news spread, a shrine would have to be built. Pilgrims would travel here to see the place where Ta No Kami had . . .

The spirit seemed to be trying to stand, but, very un-spirit-like, it was having trouble. As he tumbled forward, the sun shone on his back, illuminating a rainbow of colors. As the villagers saw it, a murmur spread through the crowd.

Now on his hands and knees, the kami splashed about, trying to rise again. Two of the elders exchanged glances. Perhaps someone should help him? No, that would be . . . blasphemous.

The kami got to his feet and took a few steps forward, clumsily, like a baby. The sun illuminated the front of his body now, and the villagers could see something that looked very much like blood. But that was unthinkable, unless it was meant to be a bad omen.

A very bad omen.

There was only one other explanation. One of the elders took a breath and stepped into the rice paddy, thinking that if he were

wrong, he would be struck dead. That would not be so bad, because he had already lived a long time. Besides, death was certain to be swift.

But nothing happened. Ankle deep in the water of the paddy, the elder turned and said, "Come and help me. If it is only a man, we cannot let him die in the rice field." Everyone saw the truth of this. Death brought pollution to the place where it occurred. Even Buddhist monks would have to work hard to make the paddy safe for planting again. Perhaps it could not be used this year at all.

The kami—or man, for that is what he turned out to be after all—had fallen again, and was lying with his face down, motionless. "Lift him up! Lift him up!" the elder called to the others. "He must not die here."

There was no lack of helpers. Now that others saw it was safe to enter the paddy, many followed. As they pulled the fallen man from the muddy water, they saw that he was bleeding from several gashes in his chest and arms. But his back was what caused the greatest surprise among those who picked him up. They had seen tattoos before, but none as elaborate and colorful as the one this man had. It was almost enough to make them think he was, after all, a visitor sent from heaven to deliver some strange and wonderful message—one that only a very wise man could decipher.

1 —
The Tattooed Man

*I*t is fortunate," Seikei said, "that you were visiting this province."

His foster father, Judge Ooka, gave a modest smile. The two of them were on horseback, riding slowly because the road here was so seldom used that it was strewn with loose stones and branches. "Fortunate for whom?" the judge asked.

"Well . . ." Seikei hesitated, sensing that the judge was testing his ability to reason. "The person who was killed?" That sounded wrong as soon as he said it.

"We do not know yet if he was killed," the judge pointed out. "The only information we have is that a man was attacked. A serious attack evidently, but perhaps he is still alive. And if he *does* prove to be dead, I can hardly think him fortunate, whether or not we arrive."

"Then you will find out who killed him."

"Perhaps so."

"I am sure you will, Father. The provincial governor told us it was a small village, fewer than a hundred people."

"Are you suggesting that those are the only suspects?"

"It seems likely, doesn't it? There seem to be no other people living nearby." Seikei motioned to the woods and mountains that flanked the lonely road.

"On the other hand," the judge reasoned, "this incident will cause quite severe hardship for all the villagers. It disrupted their rice-planting ceremony, and they fear it will drive away the Ta No Kami. The rice crop will then fail, and they will go hungry, even starve. Who among them would desire such misery?"

"That is why the governor asked *you* to solve the crime," said Seikei. After a moment's thought, he added, "So it is the *villagers* who are fortunate you were visiting the area."

"I hope I can justify your confidence," said the judge.

Seikei had no doubt he would. Throughout Japan, the judge was well known for his uncanny ability to solve the most difficult crimes. The *shogun* himself had placed the judge in charge of keeping order in Edo, the capital of the *bakufu*, the samurai government. Two years ago, through good fortune, Seikei had helped the judge solve the mystery of a stolen jewel. That had allowed Seikei to achieve his lifelong dream of becoming a samurai. His original father had been a tea merchant, and in the ordinary course of things that would have been Seikei's destiny as well. But the judge, seeing Seikei's qualities, had adopted him and

given him the training that the son of a samurai family should have.

Seikei and the judge had traveled here, to a province in the north, on a mission for the shogun. The judge was to examine the records of the local rice tax revenues, which were unusually low. Seikei knew that the real reason the judge wanted to come here was that the coastal waters were full of *shirao*—tiny fish that were netted and then eaten while still alive. The judge was a connoisseur of fine food, as anyone seeing his stocky frame could guess.

The judge had found the shirao delicious. So, as a courtesy to the local governor, he had agreed to investigate the mysterious attack on a man during the spring rice-planting festival in an outlying village.

It was truly not much of a village, Seikei thought as they saw it from the crest of a hill. It was more like a collection of ramshackle straw-roofed huts that looked as if they had been built close to each other by accident. He sensed that people were watching them from the dark interiors of the huts. A small boy ran across the road in front of them as if he were fleeing demons. The people here probably saw very few strangers, Seikei thought. Any samurai who passed through were likely to be *ronin*, masterless warriors who preyed on the farmers more often than they protected them.

A man suddenly emerged from the house where the little boy had gone. He was quite old, and rested his hand on the boy's shoulder to steady himself. A smile showed

only two teeth. With difficulty, he approached and bowed deeply before the judge.

Dismounting more easily than anyone might have thought possible, given his rotund belly, the judge returned the bow. Seikei could see on the old man's face the surprise such a courteous gesture caused—especially coming from a samurai.

When the judge announced his name, the old man's eyes widened still further. Even here, thought Seikei, they have heard of Judge Ooka.

"We are honored," said the man, who gave his name only as Higo. In villages like this, a single name was sufficient. It was clear he was the village headman. "Surely you have not come all the way from Edo."

"No," said the judge. "My son and I were here on business."

"Then we will not waste your valuable time," said Higo. "But I have forgotten my manners. Would you like some tea to refresh yourself?"

"After we look at the man who was attacked," said the judge. "If he is still alive," he added.

"He is breathing," said Higo, nodding. "But that is the only sign of life."

The villagers had carried the man to a small hut that was otherwise used for storage. No one wanted to have a stranger die in their house, thought Seikei. If so they would have to pay a monk to perform the rites of purification. Still, someone had covered the man's wounds with cloths

and provided a blanket to keep him warm. No doubt there were herbs under the cloths, for even a small village would have someone who knew medicine.

Seikei had to look closely before he could see the man's chest move up and down. It didn't appear that he would be breathing much longer. The judge told Seikei to roll up the bamboo shade that covered the window. Then he leaned over and lifted one of the man's hands. He motioned Seikei to look. At first, the only thing Seikei noticed was that the top joint on his little finger was missing. There were also a few cuts, no doubt the result of a struggle with his attacker. Then the judge spread the man's fingers. On the folds between each were faint marks—old tattoos. They formed three characters: *ya-ku-za*, the symbols for the numbers eight, nine and three.

What could that mean? Seikei looked at the judge, who had a little smile on his face but did not offer an explanation.

Higo, the village headman, had also remained silent till now. But he seemed to feel that there was something more important to show the judge. He removed the blanket and said to Seikei, "Help me turn him over."

Seikei wasn't eager to touch the man, but the judge gave him a nod. Surprisingly, the body was harder to move than Seikei had thought. The man was heavy.

The sight of his back made Seikei gasp. Every part of his skin, from his neck to his buttocks, had been tattooed. Nothing as dull as the few characters between his fingers.

Spread out before them was a whole scene, like the nature prints sold in Edo for people to display in their houses. In the scene on the man's back, a mountain towered over a valley through which a stream flowed. Seikei could see little details: trees, rock formations, pinecones, wildlife. He caught his breath as he thought of how long it must have taken for the tattoo to be completed. The precise lines were unwavering, indicating that the man had not flinched as the needles made their way through his flesh.

The judge, as usual, saw something more. He touched a spot on the man's skin where a footpath had been drawn. It had a series of symbols on it, like arrows pointing, but not exactly. The judge traced the path as it moved from one side of the man's back to the other.

"Do you have paper?" he suddenly asked Seikei.

He did. As the judge knew well, Michiko, the daughter of a papermaker, regularly sent Seikei gifts of fine writing paper. She was grateful that Seikei had once spoken up to save her father from a false accusation. That incident had actually brought Seikei good fortune, for it was then that the judge had first noticed him.

The village headman showed Seikei where to find water, and he mixed some fresh ink with the kit he always carried. "I have no colors," he told the judge. "Only black." The tattoo itself was brilliantly colored.

"That will have to do," said the judge. "Make a copy of this scene as carefully as you can. Be sure, especially along the path, to copy exactly what is there."

As Seikei set to work, the judge and the headman went outside. Seikei tried to concentrate on his drawing, but questions kept popping into his head. What had caused the judge to think that this tattoo was important? Seikei had seen tattoos before, but they were almost always on the bodies of men who worked at "naked jobs"—tasks for which they shed most of their clothing. *Kago*-bearers decorated their bodies this way; so did carpenters, gardeners, messengers and even firemen. But farmers never did. They led simple lives. A tattoo would seem merely like a wasted expense. Anyone displaying such an elaborate design on his body would have stood out in an isolated place like this.

Seikei studied the work he had done so far. Without the colors of the original, a pattern began to emerge. The path that the judge had traced with his finger now seemed the centerpoint of the scene. Everything in nature around it seemed placed very specifically, as if they were meant as signposts. Landmarks.

Could this be a map? But what did it show? Some place around here? The mountains looked more like those in the far west. The path . . . where was it intended to lead someone?

Seikei was still puzzling over these questions when the judge returned. "Have you finished?" he asked.

"Nearly," said Seikei, concentrating on his work. The judge had always told him not to hold back any suggestions, so he added, "It looks to me as if this might be a map."

11

"An excellent observation," the judge responded. "But it seems to be only part of a map."

Seikei nodded. That still left many questions. "Where is the rest of it? And why would anybody tattoo a map on a man's back?"

"I thought we might answer those questions when we found the person who attacked this man," said the judge. "But I was too optimistic."

Seikei let this sink in. "You have found that person already?"

"The villagers were afraid of the wrath of the rice kami when the wounded man broke up their ceremony," explained the judge. "So they did not go back to further examine the rice paddy. Just now, with the help of the headman and his sons, we found the body of the attacker." He nodded toward the wounded man. "He defended himself quite well."

"He killed the man who attacked him? How?"

"Apparently by holding him under water until he drowned," the judge replied. "That was particularly impressive, considering that the attacker was dressed as a ninja."

A ninja! One of the hereditary assassins who went about their deadly business nearly unseen. Some people thought they were figures of myth, but Seikei knew differently. He looked at the unconscious man with new respect. Seikei himself had once managed to defeat a ninja, but not in hand-to-hand combat. Now he noticed that even though

the unconscious man was middle-aged, he had maintained his youthful strength. Beneath the tattoo was a muscled torso.

"What should we do with him?" Seikei asked.

"Better not to move him," said the judge. "If he survives, he will be able to answer questions. I've sent a message to the governor to send guards here."

"You think he is still in danger?" Seikei asked. "Even when the man who attacked him is dead?"

The judge looked down at the man. "He still has the map," he said.

2 —

EIGHT, NINE AND THREE

*T*he villagers looked unhappy as Seikei and the judge prepared to leave. Now that they were no longer under suspicion, some of them had emerged from their homes to get a glimpse of the shogun's most trusted official.

"They blame me for being the one who discovered the dead body in the rice paddy," the judge explained to Seikei. "Now they will need to pay a Buddhist monk to purify the field, and delay planting their crop."

"But the dead man would have been there whether you discovered him or not," Seikei said.

"If he had not been discovered, however, a great deal of trouble would have been avoided," replied the judge. "Most people, I have found, would rather avoid trouble than make sure the correct thing is done. They probably also wish they hadn't bound up the wounds of the man with the tattoo."

Two samurai had arrived to guard the unconscious man,

but they weren't very happy either. In such an out-of-the-way spot, it seemed unlikely that they would have an opportunity to do anything useful. And the food would be much worse than they normally enjoyed at the governor's headquarters. "How long do you want us to stay here?" one of them had asked the judge.

"Until the man dies or awakens," the judge told him. "If he becomes well enough to travel, bring him to me in Edo."

"Edo?" The samurai's face brightened at the thought of traveling to the shogun's capital city. There were many opportunities in Edo for a samurai to advance his career—and, as Seikei knew well, plenty of entertainment as well, if that was what you wanted. This samurai looked as if he were thinking of the entertainment.

"The officials at the shogun's palace will know where to find me," the judge said. The guard looked impressed and promised to carry out his orders.

As Seikei and the judge prepared to mount their horses, Seikei asked, "Do you think the man will get better?"

"He is strong," said the judge, "but I think it is more likely that someone else will come looking for that map."

"Do you know why they want it?"

"Not yet. But the marks on the man's hands indicate that he is—or once was—a criminal."

"Ya-ku-za? What does that mean?" Seikei knew what the numbers were, but not why they marked the man as a criminal.

"Are you familiar with the card game *sammai karuta?*"

"Three-card? My brother used to play it with his friends. Sometimes they even gambled coins." Seikei bit his lip. The only time he had taken part in a game, he had lost money that he had intended to use to buy a book.

"As you recall," the judge went on, "the object is to draw cards that add up to nineteen, or at least higher than any other player, without going over nineteen."

"Yes."

"Well, *ya*, eight, *ku*, nine, and *za*, three, add up to twenty."

"A losing hand," said Seikei. He knew about losing hands. He had lost five times in a row before his money was gone.

"Quite so. That is why many criminals use it as a code among themselves. They are, in the end, always losers."

"And this man . . . was part of the *yakuza?*"

"Or still is."

"Why are we going to Edo, then?"

"Because I want to learn more about the map."

That would be difficult, thought Seikei. Edo had more than a million people in it. Not even the shogun knew exactly how many.

"Take good care of the copy you made," said the judge. "We will need it."

It occurred to Seikei that someone might come in search of *that* as well.

— ◂ ◂ ◂

Three days later, back in Edo, Seikei discovered why the judge needed the copy of the map. The two of them were walking through a section of the city where Seikei had never been before. Most of the people here looked as if they were up to no good. Seikei saw several men skulk away when they saw the shogun's hollyhock crest on the judge's *kimono*. Unlike other parts of town, few of the shops here displayed banners advertising their wares. People did seem to be selling merchandise on the street itself, but they picked up their wares and disappeared when the judge approached.

"Why is everyone here afraid of you?" asked Seikei.

"Perhaps they think they have something to fear from an officer of the law," said the judge. "People with guilty consciences always hear footsteps behind them."

"Shouldn't we have brought Bunzo?" Seikei asked. Bunzo was the judge's chief assistant, who had trained Seikei in *bushido,* the way of the warrior. Seikei believed that Bunzo was powerful enough to protect them from an army of thieves, if necessary.

"Why?" the judge responded. "Do you feel we are in danger?"

"Not exactly. But shouldn't you arrest some of these men and see if they are criminals?"

The judge shook his head. "There is enough work in solving crimes that we *know* about. If we arrested people to find out if they had done anything wrong, where would we stop? Perhaps I would end up arresting *you*." He gave Seikei

a look that was so stern that Seikei couldn't help but laugh. But it was a weak, nervous laugh, making him sound guilty, even to himself. He looked away.

"Here is our destination," the judge said. He stopped in front of a one-story building where a small banner hung limply over the door. It read HORI-MONO, TATTOOING. The place looked flimsy enough to collapse in a strong wind. The door rattled in its frame as the judge slid it open and entered. Seikei followed.

Inside, a few burning incense sticks stood upright in bowls of sand. The scent they gave off wasn't strong enough to completely cover some other, far less pleasant, smell. Seikei tried, but failed to discern what the foul odor might be. His attention was drawn to three shelves on the wall, on which needles were displayed. They were arranged in sizes, from very thin, short ones to thick ones that looked almost wide enough to be knives.

Around the rest of the walls were drawings that displayed what Seikei assumed were tattoo styles—dragons, tigers, foxes, eagles, swords and numerous nature scenes. None was as elaborate as the one Seikei carried in his sleeve.

"Hello, Kita," said the judge. Seikei blinked, because he had not noticed anyone else in the room. On a mat in the corner, between two bowls of burning incense sticks, was what appeared to be an old kimono, carelessly dropped there. Then, it moved. The top of a head, with only a few strands of white hair, emerged from the clothing. Then

two eyes, surrounded by wrinkles. It was like watching the dawning of a very old sun.

The eyes brightened when they spotted the judge. The pile of clothing rose, though the man beneath was not much taller standing than he was sitting. He bowed deeply and said, "How may I be of service?" As he spoke, his eyes flicked over to Seikei. "You have brought me this young man, who wants a tattoo?" The man named Kita darted forward, moving faster than Seikei thought he could. He slid Seikei's sleeve halfway up, staring at his arm as if he were contemplating a splendid dinner.

Seikei pulled away, but Kita had seen enough. "You have wonderful skin," he said softly. "It would be an honor for me to turn it into a work of art."

"Kita, this is my son," the judge said.

Glancing at Seikei's two swords, Kita nodded. He couldn't hide his disappointment. "You know," he said, "it is written that long ago, samurai covered their bodies with tattoos showing their deeds of heroism."

"Not today," the judge said firmly. "We have something to show you." He nodded at Seikei, who brought out the drawing he had made. As he unrolled it, Kita's expression went through a series of changes. First curiosity, then, as he recognized it, a kind of shock. Finally, although he tried to conceal it, craftiness.

"Your honor," he said, "where have you seen this?"

"That does not concern you," said the judge. "Do you recognize the style?"

"It is unmistakable," Kita responded. "A great master of the art created this." He looked at the drawing longingly. "I would like to see the original."

"A name, if you please," said the judge.

"Oh, certainly this is Tengen's work," Kita said. "You see the way the slope of the rocks is depicted with sharp, thin lines? Only he—"

"Yes," interrupted the judge. "And where is Tengen now?"

"He is where all of us will go in due course," said Kita. "With his ancestors."

The judge nodded. "Where did he practice his trade?"

"His art," Kita corrected. "He began in the far west. I believe he did some work in Yamaguchi province, at the end of the Inland Sea. But when he started to gain fame, he opened an establishment here in Edo. Actually . . ." Kita hesitated.

"Yes?" the judge prompted.

"He had an apprentice," Kita said with a sniff. "A man of little talent."

"What is his name?"

"You wouldn't learn anything from him."

"Much of my time is wasted, I admit," said the judge. "I just like to satisfy my curiosity."

"Shotaro," Kita said. "I think that was his name."

"Where can I find him?"

"I really don't know. He's not someone I regard as a competitor."

The judge looked around. "You know, Kita, this shop of yours is not well constructed. With all these incense sticks, I think it could be regarded as a fire hazard."

"Everybody burns incense sticks," Kita protested.

"Still, it is my duty as head of the Edo fire brigade to be alert to dangerous situations. If I decide your shop is a fire hazard, I must send some men to pull it down. That would be a shame, of course, but—"

"You can find Shotaro at a small establishment on Nakabashi Street, near the river," Kita said.

"Your cooperation is appreciated," said the judge.

Kita gave a bow. "I should tell you that Shotaro is seldom there. He's not much of a worker."

"Then I hope we will be fortunate enough to find him in," said the judge.

After they left the shop, the judge took Seikei by the arm. "Conceal yourself over there," he said, pointing to some crates piled in the street. "Wait until Kita emerges from his shop and follow him."

Seikei nodded. "Do you think he will try to warn this Shotaro that we are looking for him?"

"No. I think he may go in a different direction, toward our real prey."

"Who is that?"

"That's your job. When you find out, come and tell me. I will be at the hunting grounds at the shogun's palace. Oh, and give me the copy of the tattoo that you made."

Seikei wondered why the judge would want to go hunting at this time, but he did as he was told. Sure enough, only moments after the judge had disappeared down the street, Kita emerged from his shop. After a furtive look around, he moved off in the other direction. Seikei followed.

3 —
THE UNDERGROUND MAN

Kita seemed to be heading for the waterfront, down at the edge of Edo Bay. Because the streets were narrow and winding, Seikei had to stay closer to him than he would have liked. In any case, Kita did not appear to have any idea he was being followed. Speed seemed to be his main goal. The old man moved more nimbly than Seikei would have thought possible.

The buildings here were mostly old warehouses. Some appeared to be deserted. Seikei recalled that the judge had said such abandoned places should be pulled down to prevent fires from sweeping out of control.

He strained his eyes to keep Kita in sight. The tattooist's dusty clothing seemed to blend in with the surroundings. Then, abruptly, he dropped from sight altogether.

Seikei blinked and ran to the spot where he had last seen Kita. There was nothing here but a rickety bamboo

wall, once painted red but now holding only a few remaining specks of color. Seikei pulled at it, searching for some kind of doorway. But the entrance, if there was one, seemed to be somewhere else.

Then he stumbled over something and looked down. At his feet was a heavy iron ring. Faintly, Seikei could see the outline of a trapdoor that must have once been used as a way to unload goods directly into the cellar of the building. A thin slab of rock covered the trapdoor, making it appear as if it were part of the street.

Seikei pulled on the ring, and the door rose easily, exposing a narrow flight of stairs leading into a black hole.

He hesitated. The judge had told him to find out who Kita went to see. It was Seikei's duty to follow, wherever he went. Yet perhaps it might be better to report first and see—

Before Seikei could decide, someone shoved him from behind, and he went tumbling headlong into the inky darkness.

The next thing he knew, he opened his eyes and found himself in a stuffy room lit only by a few candles. His head hurt, but when he tried to rub it, he found that his hands were bound behind his back.

Seikei was in a sitting position; someone had propped him against a wall. He gradually became aware that a middle-aged man sat staring at him from the other side of the room. He wore a plain kimono, the color of stone. His

face was lined and his brow furrowed as if he were thinking of some problem.

"Feeling better now?" he asked. "You took a nasty fall." He sounded concerned.

"Someone pushed me," Seikei said. "Was it you?"

"No. Just someone I keep around to make sure I don't have unexpected visitors. I seldom do, but apparently Kita was careless when he entered." The man shook his head. "Perhaps it was for the best."

"Why do you say that?" Seikei asked. He tested the bonds that held his hands. They weren't very tight, and perhaps he could work himself free.

"You needn't struggle," the man said. "Someone will free you in a little while. I know you're Judge Ooka's son, and I have no intention of incurring his wrath."

Seikei wondered momentarily how the man knew that but then realized Kita must have told him. "Who are you?" Seikei asked. "Where is Kita?"

"People call me Rofu. As for Kita, he's gone. He was horrified when he saw you. Thought you were dead, at first."

"I *could* have been killed," Seikei said.

"If I wanted you dead," Rofu said calmly, "you would have been dead by now."

"So why have you tied me up?"

"Well, you wear swords, you see, and like many young men you might be prone to act rashly. Someone could have gotten hurt."

"Now that you've made that clear," said Seikei, "why don't you just let me go?"

"Because I have some other things I want to clear up. Can I trust that you will take a message to your father?"

"You may rely on it," said Seikei. "Perhaps I should do it right now."

"Not just yet," said Rofu. "I understand that you have a copy of a tattoo that was on a man's back."

Seikei tried to recall what the judge had told Kita. He hadn't said anything about *where* the tattoo had been. "It was a copy of a tattoo," Seikei said carefully.

"But you do not seem to have it now. Pardon my curiosity, but I had someone search you."

Seikei fought back his anger. "That's right," he told Rofu. "I no longer have it."

"Too bad," Rofu said. "Could you describe the man whose skin bore this tattoo?"

Seikei hesitated. Obviously Rofu knew more about the man than he let on. Perhaps to gain information from him, Seikei should cooperate.

Abruptly Rofu rose to his feet. Seikei tensed, feeling how helpless he was.

But Rofu only bent over and showed Seikei his hands. "Did he have marks like these?" he asked.

Seikei saw the numbers tattooed between Rofu's fingers: ya-ku-za. Slowly, he nodded.

Rofu seemed satisfied, for the time being. He returned to his mat across the room and sat. Though his eyes were

on Seikei, they seemed focused on something else. The candles flickered as if a breeze had blown through, but that was impossible.

After a while Rofu seemed to have made up his mind. "The judge must know that it is dangerous to possess that map," he said.

Seikei didn't reply. He was pretty sure that the judge had not told Kita that the tattoo was part of a map.

"Otherwise," Rofu continued, "he would not have taken it from you."

"Or he didn't want it to fall into the wrong hands," Seikei suggested.

Rofu smiled, revealing that he had several missing teeth. "You have paper and a brush in your sleeve," he said.

Seikei was a little startled till he recalled that he had been searched. Resentful, he refused to reply, but Rofu went on: "Was it you who made the copy of the tattoo?"

Seikei kept his silence, but Rofu nodded. "I am going to show you something," he said. "Something I usually go to great lengths to conceal."

Seikei looked around the underground room, expecting to spot a strongbox or locked chest in which Rofu kept precious objects.

Instead, Rofu moved the candles closer to himself, lining them up carefully in two rows. Then he turned his back on Seikei and untied his kimono. As the back of the garment slid down, Seikei's jaw fell with it.

Rofu's back held another tattoo, the colors just as

shimmering as the other, even in the candlelight. It was not exactly the same as the first one, Seikei saw. There were different landmarks, though the path still led from one side of the image to the other. But the strange symbol that pointed out the direction one should travel was here too.

"Was the tattoo you saw before like this one?" Rofu asked.

"Yes," Seikei admitted.

"Kita told me," said Rofu. "It hardly seemed possible. After what happened to Boko, the rest of us understood that it was dangerous to let people know what was on our backs." He pulled up the back of his kimono and turned to face Seikei again.

"Who is Boko?" Seikei asked.

"Someone else who had one of these tattoos," said Rofu. "He's dead now. Did you see this *other* tattoo on a dead man?"

Seikei hesitated before deciding it was all right to answer. "He was not dead, but unconscious. He had been attacked."

Rofu fell silent, as if pondering what Seikei had told him. "Was this in Edo?" he asked finally.

"No. It was in a farm village in a northern province."

"That must have been Tatsuo. He was the only one I lost track of completely. Did he have a joint missing from his left little finger?"

"Yes."

"He lost it in a wager. I wonder how she found him."

"The person who attacked him was a man," said Seikei. "*His* body was found later."

Rofu shook his head as if that didn't matter. "Would you like to make a copy of my tattoo, as you did Tatsuo's?"

The offer surprised Seikei. "I thought you said it was dangerous to let people know about the tattoo."

"Well, you already know, don't you? I suppose you would want to show it to your father?"

Seikei nodded.

Rofu smiled again. "Very good. Most people would have lied to me. Now, there's just one other thing."

Just one? Seikei had a hundred questions he wanted to ask.

"Obviously I must untie your hands so you can draw," said Rofu. "So I must have your promise that you will not try to use your swords instead of your brush."

Seikei thought. "My father will want to question you," he said.

"I suppose he will," said Rofu. "You can always bring him back here."

Somehow Seikei suspected that if he did, Rofu would have departed.

"The alternative," Rofu said, "is that I leave now, and you will not have the opportunity to copy the tattoo."

"And perhaps no one will find me," said Seikei.

"With time, you will work your way out of those bonds. I can see you straining at them already."

"So why should you let me copy your tattoo at all? Why *not* just leave?"

"Let me say only that I have a reason. Perhaps you will discover it," Rofu said. "For your sake, I hope not."

4 —
A Dishonorable Weapon

*W*hen Seikei emerged from the trapdoor in the street, he was surprised to find that it was still light outside. Below ground it had been impossible to tell how much time had passed. He headed in the direction of the shogun's palace, eager to report to the judge.

Unfortunately, Rofu had refused to answer any more of Seikei's questions. All he would say was, "I think you will find that too much information is dangerous." A puzzling statement, Seikei thought. Wouldn't it be safer if he knew who wanted the men with these maps, and why? That way he could discover where the danger came from. In response to all these arguments, Rofu had merely smiled.

But now, as Seikei made his way through the streets, he had a strange feeling. He reached inside his sleeve to make sure the rolled-up copy of the tattoo he had just made was still there. He looked over his shoulder, but no one behind him seemed to be observing him. Yet the feel-

ing remained—a very distinctive one, like the taste of something eaten only once, but never forgotten.

Where had he felt it before?

When the memory came back to him, he stopped in his tracks.

It had been on the sacred mountain of Miwayama, above the O-Miwa shrine. The monks who tended the shrine had allowed Seikei to climb the mountain to find the ninja who had killed Lord Kira. To do so, he had followed the tracks of a fox to a cave where the ninja was sleeping. Seikei had felt then the way he did now.

He hurried on, faster now, though he knew that if it was Kitsune the ninja who pursued him, Seikei could not escape by hurrying.

Soon, though, the feeling disappeared, like a cloud that darkens the sky for a moment and then moves on. Perhaps it was just the excitement Seikei felt at helping solve another case that had awakened that memory.

Perhaps.

At the shogun's castle, Seikei passed through the entryway quickly, for the guards recognized him as the judge's son. It was still a long walk to the hunting grounds, for the castle complex consisted of many buildings. It was not only the residence of the shogun Yoshimune and his family, but also the home of hundreds of samurai retainers and guards. The stables alone had space for more than five hundred horses.

The grounds were also crisscrossed with moats, created

long ago to keep out invading armies. In fact, in the decades since the current shogun's ancestor Tokugawa Ieyasu had made the castle his headquarters, no one had successfully attacked the castle. Though the emperor in Kyoto was officially the ruler of Japan, the shogun's bakufu, military government, held the real power.

Beyond the castle complex was a garden that provided a place for the shogun's family to enjoy views that changed with the seasons. Seikei passed that, for the trees were still bare this early in spring, and came to a wilder area. Here the grass was left to grow long, and trees provided a habitat for the birds, deer and other animals that roamed here. These were the private hunting grounds of the shogun and his guests.

Seikei spotted the judge, his chief aide Bunzo and another samurai standing in a cleared space. As he drew nearer, he saw that the third man held a strange-looking object. It seemed to be a long metal tube with a wooden handle at one end. Though Seikei had never seen such a thing before, something about it seemed familiar. Then he realized it was shaped like the unusual symbol on the maps that pointed the way to some destination.

The judge smiled when he saw Seikei approach. "I can see that you have news for me," he said.

Seikei realized the look on his face showed his eagerness. "I found a second person with a map on his back," he said. No need to add, at least while Bunzo was here, that he had been bound and helpless when he made this dis-

covery. He took the copy of the map from his sleeve and unrolled it.

After a brief examination the judge said, "It appears that there must be more of these. The edges of this one do not merge with the other map."

Seikei nodded. "Rofu, the man with this one, told me the name of a third person who had one. But that man is now dead, and Rofu didn't tell me how many there were originally."

"Where is this Rofu?" asked the judge.

"He was in a . . . room underneath the street near the waterfront," Seikei replied. "I could not persuade him to come with me."

"There are many tunnels there to provide drainage at high tide," the judge said. "Criminals frequently use them as hiding places."

"He had the ya-ku-za tattoo between his fingers," said Seikei. "Do you think the map might show where these criminals hid their loot?"

"If that was all it showed, I would not have bothered with it," said the judge. "I fear it is the key to something far more troubling." He pointed to the mark on the map and then to the odd-looking object the other samurai held. "You see the resemblance between these two things?"

Seikei nodded. The judge turned toward the other samurai, a tall thin man with lined hollows in his cheeks, and said, "Reijo, may I present my son to you." Seikei bowed as the man acknowledged him with a nod.

"Reijo is the shogun's keeper of arms," the judge explained. "He is going to demonstrate the use of this instrument. It is called a musket."

They were standing at the top of a grassy slope. At the bottom, Seikei saw, was another man with a cage of birds. At Reijo's signal, the man took one of the birds from the cage and tossed it into the air.

Freed, the bird spread its wings and tried to fly off. Reijo raised the musket, and almost at once it made a loud noise that caused Seikei to clap his hands over his ears. Evidently it disturbed the bird as well, for it stopped flying and fell to the ground.

Reijo led the way as the four of them walked to the spot where the bird lay. Seikei was astounded. It was dead, bleeding from a wound. "How did—?" he began, but then realized Reijo would explain.

The samurai opened a small leather bag tied around his waist. It was full of metal pellets. He took one and, using a thin rod attached to the musket, forced it into the bottom of the metal tube. Then, from another bag, he took a small paper capsule and slipped it into a hole in the top of the tube. Finally, he poured a small quantity of black powder into a small shallow cup on the side of the tube.

He turned to Seikei and pointed to a small curved stick along the side of the tube. "Notice," Reijo said, "that the tip of it is burning." Seikei nodded, seeing the slight trail of smoke that arose from it.

"Now," said Reijo, "when I pull this small lever under

the barrel, it releases the part with the burning tip. When it touches the powder, it burns more quickly and the fire spreads inside the barrel, causing an explosion that sends the pellet out of the barrel at a high speed. So fast you cannot even see it."

"That was how you killed the bird?" Seikei asked.

"Yes. It is not so easy as it first seems, however. It requires practice to hit something as small and swift as a bird. Muskets are much better suited for battle, where your opponent is large and slow."

"You mean . . . this could kill a man?" The metal pellets seemed so tiny.

"Most certainly," said Reijo.

"From a distance as far as you were from the bird?"

"Or even farther. Farther than an ordinary man could shoot an arrow."

"What a dishonorable way of fighting that would be," said Seikei. "Not to face your enemy, but to sneak up on him like a thief."

Reijo looked uncomfortable and glanced at the judge, who seemed to be trying to conceal a smile. "Actually, Seikei," the judge said, "the shogun's ancestor Ieyasu armed some of his men with muskets like this one."

Seikei felt his face redden. "I did not know that," he admitted. "But why do we not use them now?"

"After taking control of Japan, Ieyasu felt that such weapons were . . . perhaps too powerful. They were originally brought here from the barbarian nations."

"The ones whose ships are allowed to land only at Deshima?"

The judge nodded. "Apparently in the countries from which these ships come, warfare using such weapons is quite common."

"Truly, they are barbarians."

"And that is one reason why the shoguns ever since have carefully restricted any trade with those countries. However, as you recall from our trip to Osaka, there are smugglers who violate the shogun's laws."

Seikei had helped the judge expose a band of these smugglers, although ultimately they escaped. "You think Captain Thunder and his men are smuggling these muskets?" Seikei asked.

"I don't believe so," the judge said. "They were working merely for money. What we are seeing now is far more dangerous. For years there have been rumors that one or more of the *daimyo* lords have secretly been purchasing these weapons from barbarians. Some of the outer lords—those who were among the last to surrender to Ieyasu—never became truly loyal to the shogun."

"But isn't that why they must live in Edo with their families one year out of every two?"

The judge nodded. "It helps to ensure their loyalty. But that may not stop some from plotting against the shogun anyway. When I first saw the tattoo on the back of the unconscious man in Echigo province, I was struck by the mark used to point out what direction the path followed. I

had seen muskets before. But an ordinary person, even a criminal, would not know what a musket is. Whoever put it on the tattoo must have had a reason."

Seikei thought. "Kita, the tattoo artist, told us the man who drew the tattoo is now dead. Do you believe him?"

"Believe no one until you have confirmed what they say," the judge replied. "Which is what we will try to do now."

5 —
The Monkey Thief

After Seikei explained where Rofu's hideout was, the judge sent Bunzo to take him into custody, if possible. "Likely not," the judge admitted. "Since he refused to answer your questions, he will try to elude us. As will Kita. We can get no more information from him. Yet Bunzo is resourceful, and may find something of interest."

Seikei then told the judge the whole story, admitting that for a while he had been Rofu's prisoner. "All the more reason why he would not want to fall into my hands," said the judge. "You and I have another errand."

Seikei followed as the judge made his way to the section of the city where Kita had said Shotaro worked. In the first tattoo parlor they entered, the proprietor said that Shotaro was no longer in business. "I can do a better job than he," the man said. "What kind of tattoo did you want?"

"It's not for us," the judge said. He nodded, and Seikei unrolled the copies he had made of the two tattoos.

"That's Tengen's work," the man said. "He was truly an artist."

"We understood that Shotaro was his apprentice," said the judge.

"True enough, showing only that one can be a great artist and yet not a good judge of others' talent. He was unable to pass his skills on to Shotaro." The man took another look at the two copies. "You know," he said slowly, "I think I've seen another tattoo like these. They seem to be part of a series, don't they?"

"We believe so," said the judge. "Where did you see this other tattoo?"

The man hesitated. "I'm not . . . I'm not really sure it was what you are looking for."

"If it's not, no harm done," said the judge pleasantly. "There may be a reward for the man who has it, however. Tell us what you know."

"A reward? Are you sure? You see, the person who has it . . . wouldn't want to get into trouble."

"There's no crime in having a tattoo," said the judge.

"No, but there seems to be some fear that this one can bring trouble," the man said. "Truth is, the only reason I know about it is that the person came to me to see if it could be removed."

"The tattoo?"

"Yes."

"Did he say why?"

"No. He was very secretive about it. Just said it was a re-

minder of a time he wanted to forget. I thought that was peculiar. Because if it's on his back, he never has to look at it, does he?"

"Perhaps he's married now, has children."

"Not this fellow. He's a street entertainer, sleeps at a Buddhist temple, where he gets something to eat as well."

"Where is this?"

The man hesitated, looking at the judge's swords. "Excuse me for speaking frankly, sir, but he'll be wary of you."

"Because I'm a samurai? Edo is full of samurai."

"Rather because you are an official of the shogunate."

The judge's kimono was decorated with the shogun's hollyhock crest. He turned to Seikei, who wore only a plain outfit. "It seems that you would be more persuasive than I," the judge said. "I hope this time you won't need to be captured to obtain what we are trying to find out."

"I'll be careful," said Seikei. He turned to the tattooist. "What does this man look like?" he asked.

"He has a monkey," the man replied. "Usually they perform down the street where the Pure Land Temple is."

"And does he have tattoos between his fingers?"

"Yes. How did you know?"

"He's part of a club."

Outside, the judge told Seikei to return to the judge's mansion after he questioned the man. "If you can persuade him to talk, ask him how many maps there were originally. And you'd better give the two copies to me before you go."

Seikei handed them over, but his reluctance showed. "Perhaps if he saw these, he would be more willing to reveal his," he said.

"From the little we have learned so far," the judge replied, "people think it is dangerous to possess even one of these. I think it better if you avoid that danger for now. Be wary of anyone else who might be following the same path you are."

"You mean—"

"We became involved because a man was attacked. There is no reason not to believe others might be attacked as well."

"The man who was attacked in Echigo killed his assailant."

"Who, apparently, was a ninja. As you know, ninjas do not act on their own."

That was true. When Seikei had last faced a ninja—the man called Kitsune—it was to find out who had paid him to murder a daimyo. Ninjas were trained killers, willing to undertake any task and—some said—possessed of supernatural powers. Seikei shivered as he remembered the odd feeling he had experienced after leaving Rofu's hideout. He had no wish to encounter a ninja again.

After leaving the judge, he forced himself to walk steadily down the street. If something was following him, he would outdistance it.

The street widened in front of the Pure Land Temple, providing a space for entertainers and sellers of goods.

Seikei stopped to take in the crowded scene. Three musicians, each with a different-size drum, accompanied by another with a variety of gongs, provided a background theme to the activities. A juggler maintained five balls in the air at one time, and a family of acrobats formed a human pyramid with the youngest child (who looked as if she couldn't walk yet) at the top. Shoppers thronged the square, examining the merchandise for sale: kimonos, jewelry, fruit, tea, *tabi* sandals and the bowls of steaming hot noodles that were sold nearly everywhere in Edo.

Suddenly Seikei saw a monkey scampering around the legs of the people in the crowd. Occasionally it would stop and throw out its hands as if begging. A few people good-naturedly gave it nuts or pieces of fruit. Seikei watched it carefully, however, and saw the monkey slip its hand into a bag held by a woman who wasn't paying attention. The creature pulled out a coin and ran off, undetected. Seikei tried to follow, but couldn't get through the crowd as fast as the monkey. It soon slipped out of sight. Seikei could only continue in the direction it had been heading.

He passed through the densest part of the crowd and looked around. The monkey was nowhere to be seen. To Seikei's right was a side entrance to the temple grounds. On the left was a dingy little street that seemed utterly deserted. Ahead was a row of shops, but he could see no sign that anyone had traveled that way.

Then a man appeared at the narrow temple entrance. The first thing Seikei noticed was how short he was. The

man glanced briefly at Seikei, but then turned his attention elsewhere. He carried a small knife, but not to threaten anyone. Instead, he cut a pear in two and began to eat half of it. As he did, Seikei could see the now-familiar marks between his fingers. Here indeed was the person he was looking for.

The sight of the fruit instantly caused a chatter above them. Seikei looked up to the temple roof, spotting the monkey, which dropped into the man's arms. He gave the monkey the other half of the pear. The animal, as if paying for it, handed him the stolen coin. Contentedly, the monkey settled on the man's shoulder, enjoying his reward.

Seikei took a step forward, uncertain how to approach the man. "That's a clever monkey," he said.

The man didn't reply. His face looked as if he had endured many hardships in his life. The skin hung slackly from his skull, and even his ears seemed to droop. Only his eyes showed a flicker of wariness. Seikei had a feeling that the man was perpetually on guard against some hidden danger.

"Does he do tricks?" Seikei asked in what he hoped was a friendly manner.

"If he feels like it," the man responded.

Seikei took a coin from his sleeve and held it up. The eyes of both man and monkey followed the motion greedily.

The monkey had finished its treat by now. All at once it fell to the ground and let out a cry. It began to limp, using one leg gingerly as if he had hurt it.

Sympathetic, Seikei leaned over to see what was the matter. The monkey reached out in a flash and snatched the coin from his hand. Before Seikei could react, the monkey scampered up the side of the gate and sat on the roof, well out of reach.

"That was a trick," said the man.

Seikei didn't know whether to laugh or be angry. "That monkey could get you into trouble," he said.

"Why?" asked the man.

"Because stealing is a crime."

"Tell that to the monkey."

Seikei looked up. The monkey grinned at him.

Time to start over. "I guess you must live in the temple grounds here," Seikei said.

The man's eyes narrowed. "No harm in that either. When I have an extra coin or two, I donate it to the monks."

"Do they know the money is stolen?"

"If it is or not, I didn't steal it."

"Maybe you have something that you could sell and live . . ." Seikei was going to say "honestly," but changed his mind. ". . . differently."

"I have nothing to sell," said the man. "The monkey doesn't belong to me."

"Whose is he?"

"He's just a monkey. He's my friend. Would you sell your friend?"

"I didn't mean that you should sell it," said Seikei. "I was thinking of something else."

"What?"

"How about that tattoo you have on your back?"

The little man's reaction was swift and unexpected. He turned and ran down the narrow street opposite the temple entrance.

It took a moment for Seikei to recover and run after him. "Wait!" he called. "You have nothing to fear from—"

Something slipped between Seikei's ankles and he tripped, spreading flat on the dusty street. Scrambling to his knees, he realized that it had been the monkey who had tripped him. The creature now sat atop a pole holding a shop banner, still grinning. Seikei wished he had something to throw at it.

He brushed himself off and saw that the monkey's "friend" had disappeared. There was nothing to do but return and tell the judge of his failure.

No. An idea came to him. He walked back to the main street, looking for a shop that would have what he needed. Soon he entered one, made a purchase and emerged. The monkey, luckily, was still overhead, watching Seikei curiously.

Seikei took another coin from his pocket, held it up and walked in the direction of the monastery. It didn't take long for the monkey to appear in front of him, falling on the ground, playing the "hurt monkey" trick again. Seikei was insulted that the creature thought he would fall for that a second time.

Still, he leaned over, making sympathetic sounds, draw-

ing closer to the monkey. This time, when the creature's hand shot out for the coin, Seikei was ready. He threw his brand-new fishing net over the monkey's body. Startled, the creature's first reaction was to try to jump into the air. That only encircled him further in the webbing, and Seikei pulled it tight.

The monkey screeched with rage and tried to bite Seikei, but he was well trapped. "Now," Seikei said, "let's see how badly your friend wants to have you back."

6 —
Seven Men, Seven Maps

"Did you bring something for your dinner?" Bunzo asked. Seikei carried the netted monkey into the official residence the judge used in Edo. He had a larger, more comfortable estate outside the city, which he preferred. But his duties required him to stay here most of the time.

"This is a monkey that has been trained to steal," Seikei said. He set it on the floor. "I'm hoping its owner—that is, the man who uses him—will come looking for it. I told a monk at the temple where he stays how to find me."

"You can't keep it in that net," Bunzo commented. "Monkeys die if they can't get exercise."

"Well, how else can I stop it from running away?" Seikei asked.

Bunzo went somewhere and returned with a long strip of leather. He squatted down by the monkey, which cringed as if it feared the massive samurai. "Don't worry," Bunzo said. He scratched the monkey's back. "I won't hurt you."

To Seikei's amazement, the monkey sat quietly as Bunzo fashioned a collar from the leather and slipped it around the monkey's neck. He lifted the net and the monkey scampered toward the doorway. However, it stopped when it reached the end of its leash. "Not so fast," Bunzo said. "You'll have to be our guest for a while longer." He looked at Seikei. "We *could* just let him go, and follow him back to the man you want."

"Over the rooftops?" asked Seikei. "No, this man is a slippery one, and if you want to know the truth, Bunzo, I need you to capture him."

"What will we do with him?" Bunzo asked, taking it for granted that apprehending the man would be a simple task.

"Take him to the judge for questioning," Seikei said. "And possibly look at his back."

"Another of these fellows with the maps, eh?"

"I think so," said Seikei. "He ran away when I mentioned it."

"By the way, I went back to the place where you found the second man with a map," Bunzo said. "He had already fled, as we thought he would. But what I found in his hiding place indicates he was a small-time thief."

"What did you find?"

"A number of objects that seemed out of place. Some carvings from a Buddhist temple. Several kimonos made of fine silk that were much too good for that neighborhood. Strangest of all, there was a gold bracelet with some precious gems set in it."

"Why is that so strange? I mean, since you think Rofu is a thief anyway?"

"Much too expensive for a thief who lives in a hole in the ground. If he came across such an object, he would sell it at once."

"Maybe he stole it recently."

"No. It would have been reported. The judge would know by now."

"Why didn't Rofu take it with him if it's so valuable?"

"Too dangerous to carry around, is my guess."

Seikei recalled what Rofu had said when he let Seikei copy the map. "I have a reason. Perhaps you will discover it. For your sake, I hope not."

Mulling this over, he sat down to a light meal of rice and shellfish. He was tired and knew Bunzo could be trusted to keep watch all night if necessary. Even when Bunzo *did* sleep, Seikei thought he did it with one eye open. After reporting to the judge why there was now a monkey in the house, Seikei went to his room, removed his outer clothes and lay down to sleep.

It seemed as if he had just closed his eyes when shouts awakened him. He threw on a kimono and ran to the courtyard in back of the house. The moon was high in the sky, giving enough light for Seikei to see. Bunzo was holding the owner—the friend—of the monkey. The man's protests were of no avail—just like his efforts to run, since Bunzo was holding him high off the ground.

"I've done nothing! Let me go!" the man shouted. The

monkey was at the end of its leash, screeching and apparently ready to help his friend escape from Bunzo's grasp.

Just then, the judge arrived, carrying an oil lamp. "Silence!" he shouted, and even the monkey turned meekly quiet.

"I am Judge Ooka," Seikei's foster father announced. "May I ask who you are and why you have invaded my home?"

Seikei saw the man cringe when he learned whose house this was. "My . . . my name is Ito," he said. "I only came here to rescue Bula."

The judge's eyebrows went up. "This is Bula?" he said, gesturing toward the monkey.

Ito nodded.

"I understand you use him to steal," the judge said.

"He's . . . mischievous," Ito muttered.

"We can discuss that later," the judge replied. "Right now, I would like to see what is on your back."

Ito reacted as if he wanted to run again, but Bunzo had a firm grip on him. "What for?" he cried helplessly, his feet wriggling in the air.

"I am the shogun's officer," replied the judge. "I do not have to explain my reasons to you. Bunzo, remove his garment."

Ito's struggles only delayed the inevitable. Bunzo was twice his size, and picked him up as easily as he had lifted the monkey. "This isn't right!" Ito shouted. "What gives you the right to do this?"

"The shogun," said the judge. "The shogun decides what is right and what is not." He motioned to Bunzo, and in a moment Ito's jacket was off. They could see the tattoo, which was unmistakably a match for the others.

"Get your brush and paper," the judge told Seikei.

By the time he returned, the judge had begun to question Ito. The monkey-keeper sat on the floor now, though Bunzo stood by in case he should attempt to flee.

"Why would you allow something as elaborate as that tattoo to be put on your body?" asked the judge. At his direction, Seikei sat behind Ito and began to copy the tattoo. He glanced occasionally at the judge's face, wondering how angry he really was.

"We were paid to do it," Ito said simply. "If I were a gardener, I would plant flowers for anyone who hired me, without asking why."

"This seems considerably more drastic than planting flowers."

Ito shrugged. "We were young. The others seemed to think it was a good idea. I went along. We had already put these ya-ku-za tattoos on our hands, to show that we didn't care what others thought of us. Getting the tattoos on our backs was like that, only bigger. My friends would have made fun of me if I hadn't done it. It was kind of a dare. I didn't know . . ." He trailed off.

"How many of you were there?" The question was asked casually, but Seikei knew it was an important one.

Ito hesitated. "You'll never find them all," he said.

"Thank you for your concern," said the judge. "How many?"

"One of them is dead."

"I've heard."

"Well . . . there were seven of us, at the beginning."

Seven, Seikei thought. And this was the third map he'd copied. One man was dead. That left three more. But what if it was necessary to have all seven maps to find the hidden weapons?

The judge nodded. "Very good," he said, as if Ito was a schoolboy who had passed a test. Seikei expected him to ask now for the names of the other men who had tattoos.

Instead, he said, "Who paid you to let your back be used this way?"

Ito shook his head. "We were warned that to reveal that meant death."

"How long ago was this?" the judge asked.

"Ten years."

"Perhaps the need to keep the secret has lessened with time."

"The person who warned us is still alive, if that's what you mean."

The judge nodded. "However, he is not here."

Ito raised his head as if he were going to say something, but then decided to keep his mouth shut.

"I *am* here," the judge continued. "You are my prisoner.

I can have Bunzo use other methods to persuade you to talk. He can be quite forceful."

Seikei was a little surprised to hear the judge's threat. He often told Seikei that torture was useless in obtaining the truth, for a prisoner might say anything to halt the process. "They would only tell me what they think I want to hear, or expect to hear," the judge had said.

Of course Ito didn't know the judge's true feelings, but clearly he seemed more afraid of the person who had warned him. He only shook his head slightly in the face of the threat.

"Why did you try to have the tattoo removed?" asked the judge.

"How did you—" Ito began, but then realized that the tattoo artist must have spread the story. He sat, silent, while the judge waited patiently. Seikei saw beads of sweat break out on the man's back, even though the evening was a cool one.

Seikei put his brush down. "Are you finished?" the judge asked him.

"Yes," Seikei said.

"Again, I ask you for the name of the person who paid you," the judge said to Ito. "I cannot wait all night."

"Whatever you do to me," said Ito, "it will be no worse than my fate if I tell you."

"His name?" repeated the judge. Ito shook his head.

The judge pressed his lips together. "You are a brave man," he said, "but I wonder if you are willing to let your little friend suffer. Bunzo, take this monkey and—"

"Wait!" Ito cried as Bunzo stepped forward. "It . . . it wasn't a man who paid us."

"No?"

"It was a woman. A powerful woman. One you won't be able to . . . She'll destroy you."

"Then it's even more important to me that I know her name," the judge said.

"Lady Osuni." Ito spat it out like a challenge.

Seikei recognized the name. The Osunis were among the most powerful of the outer lords, the noble families who were among the last to surrender to Tokugawa Ieyasu, the shogun's ancestor. For that reason, the Tokugawas had always been particularly distrustful of them.

"It was ten years ago," the judge said softly, "that Lord Osuni died. It was a strange affair. He was drowned while fishing." He stopped to think. "But afterward, his body was carried off by some wild creature. Or so the story went."

"Lady Osuni thought the shogun was responsible," Ito replied. "She swore revenge. Her son was then only twelve years old, and she had to make sure he would someday inherit the Osuni lands. There was a map . . ." Ito paused and shook his head.

The judge finished the story for him. "Showing where one of the earlier Osuni lords had hidden a cache of weapons, preparing for the day when they would stage a rebellion against the shogun."

Ito stared at the judge as if he had suddenly sprouted wings and begun to fly. "How did you . . . ?"

The judge waved his hand. "I saw the mark on the map. Once I heard it was Lady Osuni's map, the rest was obvious."

"Well," said Ito, "the original map was far too dangerous to have around. After old Lord Osuni died, the shogun's officials came to examine his domain. Nothing could be held back from them. If they discovered the map, the secret would be out, and the shogun would execute everyone in the family. So . . ."

"She found seven young men willing to carry it on their backs for her."

"That's what happened."

"But wouldn't she have kept you all close?"

"All together, we might have aroused suspicions. She said she would know how to find us when the time came. We were promised another reward when she needed us, so that seemed all right. But then Boko spoiled things." Ito stopped talking and stared into the dark sky.

"Boko?" the judge prompted.

"He thought he was smarter than the rest of us."

"People who think that often do foolish things," said the judge.

A bell rang. It was the night bell at the front gate. The judge frowned. "Only bad news arrives in the middle of the night," he said. "Bunzo, see who is there."

"What about . . ." Bunzo motioned toward Ito.

"Seikei can protect me, if necessary," said the judge.

Inwardly, Seikei smiled. Though the judge looked fat

and slow, he had mastered the use of virtually every weapon available. He had once saved Seikei's life with an astonishing arrow shot.

There was no need for action. Ito merely bowed his head and waited.

When Bunzo returned, he handed the judge a piece of paper, folded and sealed with wax. The judge opened it and scanned the message quickly. He looked at Ito. "I'm afraid you will have to remain here as my guest a while longer," he said.

Ito's face fell. "What's the matter? I've told you the truth, far more than I should have."

"It's for your own good," said the judge. "Was one of your friends named Tatsuo?"

Ito's jaw dropped. By now he must have believed the judge was a magician. "Yes," he said.

"This note informs me that the men I entrusted with guarding Tatsuo were not up to the task. Someone has killed him. And stripped the skin from his back."

Ito moaned. "That's what she did to Boko."

7 —
BOKO'S FATE

*T*he night bell had awakened the judge's housekeeper, Noka. When she discovered people were up and talking, she brought *sake* and rice balls. Seeing that this made the monkey jealous, she found some lichee nuts for him.

Though the monkey was content, Ito was not. Despite the judge's assurances that he would be safe, Ito was shaking and kept glancing behind him. "Now you know why I tried to have the tattoo removed," he said. "She'll find us all."

"Lady Osuni is here in Edo," the judge said. "She is required to live in the capital every other year under the shogun's scrutiny. Tatsuo, however, was killed far away in Echigo."

"What difference does it make? She is rich. She can hire

people to do what she wants. Ninjas. They can go any-where. Even here."

A shiver went down Seikei's back. He recalled feeling the ninja's presence when he had left Rofu's lair.

"Your only hope," the judge told Ito, "is to be honest with me. I need to find the other men with the maps on their backs."

"That won't do you any good. I didn't tell you yet about Boko."

"Yes, what about him?"

"He quickly spent the money he received for allowing his back to be tattooed. So he demanded more. He had some idea that now he was like a valuable object that his owner had to take good care of. Well, the rest of us thought he was taking a chance, but then Lady Osuni's chamber-lain offered to let Boko live in the castle."

"A generous offer," said the judge.

"Yes, except that we heard no more of Boko until some-body met a tanner who lived outside the town."

"A tanner."

"Yes, I know they're outcasts—unclean people because of the work they do. Stripping animals of their hides, stretching and drying them. Putting their hands in death and blood. But one of the men in our group did business with this tanner, who told him . . ." Ito paused, unwilling to finish the story. Bunzo refilled the man's glass and mo-tioned for him to drink. That helped. Pale, he went on:

"The tanner had been called to the castle to do a job. They showed him a dead man, and—"

"The tanner was to turn the skin on his back into leather," finished the judge.

Ito nodded. "To preserve it," he added. He went silent for a moment, remembering. "That was when we knew how little our lives meant to Lady Osuni."

"How was it, then, that you came here to Edo?" the judge asked.

"I wasn't the only one." He glanced at the judge, clearly wondering how much he knew. "Edo's a big place. You'd think you could get lost here, wouldn't you?"

"Many try," the judge agreed. "Your friend Rofu thought so."

"You found Rofu?"

"Or he found us," the judge said. "He seemed to want my son to make a copy of his tattoo."

"Yes, that was Rofu's idea—that we could save ourselves by making copies of our tattoos. He thought we should all keep in touch, so that when the time came . . ." Ito trailed off.

"What time was that?" the judge asked.

"When Lady Osuni needed to reassemble the map. He thought if we stayed together, we could protect ourselves. Not everyone agreed. Tatsuo was always a loner, and now that she's killed him . . . Don't you see? The time is beginning."

"And that means she may now plan to use the weapons," said the judge. "We have no time to spare. Tell me how I can find the other men who were tattooed."

"I don't know. Maybe Rofu would know. I did see one of them at a fire in Edo. Michio is his name."

"A fire? What was he doing?"

"Helping to put it out. Joining the fire brigade was a good idea, I thought. Many of the firefighters have tattoos, so he wasn't so noticeable."

"What part of the city was this in?"

"Yotsuya, west of the castle."

The judge nodded. "Very good." He glanced at Bunzo, who nodded. It should be easy to find someone within the city's fire prevention force, which was under the judge's authority. "And the other two?" he asked Ito.

"Their names were Korin and Gaho. Korin's father was a carpenter. Probably he found work in that trade."

"Here in Edo?"

Ito shrugged. "If so, I never saw him."

"Was there anything distinctive about him?" the judge asked.

Ito looked at his hands. "Only . . ."

"Yes. The ya-ku-za tattoo. And Gaho? What was he like? Did he have a trade?"

"He was incapable of working at a trade. He liked to gamble."

"A difficult way to make a living."

"He would organize games for people who weren't used to gambling. Introduce them, provide a safe place where the shogun's officials wouldn't meddle—" Ito cut himself short, eyeing the judge to see if he was offended.

The judge simply said, "The shogun forbids gambling to prevent people from losing their money to no purpose."

"Some win," Ito said with a wry smile. "Everybody likes to hope they'll win. Hope is worth having. And people say you can gamble at Yoshiwara."

"Many rules are suspended in Yoshiwara. The shogun recognizes weakness too," said the judge. "Do you know where Gaho operated his games?"

Ito hesitated before saying, "No." Seikei could see he was lying.

"Well," said the judge. "Since you'll be staying here, you'll have time to recall."

Ito looked around him, as if he had been trapped. "Here? I don't want to stay here. I've told you everything I know."

"You'll be safe here," the judge said in a soothing tone. "I can't guarantee your safety any other place."

"I'll take that chance," said Ito. He picked up the monkey and stroked its back. "Bula and I are used to moving around. If we stay in one place, Lady Osuni will come for us."

"She can't come here," the judge said.

"But those who work for her can," insisted Ito.

The judge did not speak for a moment. Seikei could tell he was irritated, but was merely controlling himself. "Nevertheless," he said firmly, "you must stay."

Ito shook his head. "You have everything you want from me." He pointed to Seikei. "He's copied the map. That's all I have to give you."

Silently, Seikei agreed. He was tired of this ever-complaining petty thief and his monkey. Why would the judge want them in his house for a moment longer?

"But you still *carry* the map on your body," the judge explained. "I cannot allow it to fall into the wrong hands. What happened to Tatsuo could happen to you."

Reluctantly, Ito gave in, though Seikei wondered how sincere he was. "Noka will show you to your room," the judge said. "But first, I want you to look at the three maps we have already collected."

"Is that mine?" Ito asked as Seikei displayed the latest of the three copies.

"Yes."

"Odd, isn't it?" Ito said. "I have carried it for ten years, but never knew what it looked like before now."

Seikei unrolled the other two maps he had collected. Ito nodded as he saw each one.

"Now, we want to see if any of these fit together," said the judge. "Or if you recognize anything that will help us learn where this place is located."

Seikei arranged the maps in every possible order, even

turning them upside down, in an attempt to make them fit. But to no avail.

"Do you recognize any of the landmarks?" the judge asked Ito.

"They are a puzzle to me. The Osuni family had many lands."

"Very well," said the judge. "Bunzo, send some reliable men to watch over Lady Osuni's mansion in Edo. They must let us know at once if she attempts to leave the city. In the morning, you can search for this firefighter Michio."

Bunzo nodded and went to carry out the judge's orders. The judge sent Ito and the monkey off with his housekeeper.

"Are you sleepy?" the judge asked Seikei.

"No. I'm too excited," Seikei said. "I want to know how you plan to find Korin and Gaho."

"That will take some luck," said the judge, "although I have a few ideas. Right now I want you to conceal yourself outside this house and wait for Ito to escape."

"And then bring him back?"

"No. I'm afraid he is not a person one can keep cooped up—unless I simply put him in chains. Even then, we might find that the monkey can pick locks. Ito may be more useful to us by attracting someone else."

"Someone else? One of the others with maps on their backs?"

"No. I want you to follow him, but leave a distance

between you. I am interested in seeing who else may follow him."

"Should I then capture that person?" Seikei was eager to do something bold.

"No," the judge said, frowning. "Because I suspect that will be a very dangerous person indeed."

8 —
The Return of the Fox

*T*he judge was right. It didn't take very long for Ito to slip out of the house, once the lights inside were extinguished. Fortunately the moon was nearly full and Seikei had no trouble following him. Ito carried the monkey on his shoulder, making his silhouette unmistakable.

After curfew the city was patrolled by special squads of police. However, since they announced their approach by clapping wooden sticks, Ito and Seikei had time to conceal themselves in the shadows of alleyways or overhanging roofs.

Emerging slowly from the darkness after one patrol had passed, Seikei thought Ito had given him the slip. He started to hurry, but then saw a dark figure emerge from a doorway not far ahead. It wasn't a very large doorway, and Seikei was surprised anyone could have hidden there.

Then his blood ran cold as he realized the figure had

no monkey with him. It was not Ito. This new figure was harder to keep sight of. It would disappear into a dark place along the street and then not emerge where Seikei expected. Often Seikei hesitated, afraid of catching up to the other man, and that caused him to fall behind. Only occasionally now did Seikei catch any sight of Ito, but the shadowy figure seemed to be on his trail. Seikei kept trying to get close enough to identify his new quarry. The figure was dressed entirely in black: a tight-fitting *kosode* jacket and trousers. That could mean he was a ninja, but it might indicate only that he was prepared for trailing by night. He didn't wear the two swords—one long, one short— that were the mark of samurai rank. Ninjas used other weapons—silent, surprising, and as deadly as any sword.

Seikei wondered where Ito was leading them. He had thought at first that the monkey man might be heading for the temple where he usually slept, but if so, he was taking a long way around. Besides, the temple's gates would be shut tight at this hour. Where could Ito expect to find shelter or a person to take him in?

The part of the city they were in now seemed somehow familiar. Seikei realized they were close to the place where Rofu had his hiding place. What could Ito want with him? Did he know Rofu had already fled?

Seikei realized he had momentarily lost sight of the man following Ito. He strained his eyes, and then glimpsed something that made him stop in his tracks.

Out of the shadows up ahead emerged a small animal,

four-legged with a bushy tail. Not the monkey. It was unmistakably a fox.

If so, Seikei could think of only one explanation, and if he was correct, he would be foolish to take even one step farther. Yet he knew he must, and forced his feet to go faster.

Was it really possible, he asked himself, that the man following Ito was the ninja Kitsune? That would explain the strange feeling that Seikei had had when he'd left Rofu's hiding place. Kitsune had been there, watching.

Seikei rounded a corner, a little out of breath. Up ahead he saw quite clearly the man with a monkey on his shoulder. But he could also see what the man did not: gaining speed behind him was a running fox.

The monkey sensed the danger before Ito did. It screeched and stood up, but too late. The fox leaped through the air and over Ito's shoulder, taking the monkey with it.

Ito reacted much too slowly. After all, who would expect to be attacked by a fox in the middle of a city like Edo? By the time he recovered his wits, the fox was already halfway down the street, holding the screeching monkey in its jaws.

Finally, Ito began to run. Seikei followed behind, now wishing that the night patrollers would show up. He realized that he couldn't catch up to Ito the way the man was running now.

The trio in front of him rounded another corner and

the noise faded away. By the time Seikei reached the spot, there was nothing to be seen.

Seikei could hear only the sound of his own heavy breathing. The monkey had somehow been silenced. Seikei continued moving forward, more slowly now, trying desperately to see or hear anything that would give him a clue.

Up ahead was the edge of one of the moats that criss-crossed the city, designed to ward off any attackers who landed on the waterfront. Seikei stared down at the dark, foul-smelling water. Something floated there, crossing a streak of reflected moonlight, among the trash and debris that the tide would soon take out.

Something furry.

The monkey had performed his last trick.

But where was Ito? And Kitsune?

The silence was overpowering to Seikei. Shouldn't he hear *something*? Footsteps, cries of pain, shouts . . .

No. Only the faint splash of water lapping against the sides of the canal.

A sudden hunch made Seikei look up. Another object was moving on the canal, almost too far away to be noticed: a flat-bottomed wooden boat, the kind scavengers used to collect refuse and night soil. Dimly, Seikei glimpsed a figure standing in the rear, using a pole to push the craft forward. His back was turned, and Seikei could not see his face. But who else could it be but Kitsune?

Was Ito with him? If so, he must be lying on the bottom of the boat. Seikei searched the water's edge, but could see nothing to indicate what had happened to Ito.

There was nothing to do but return to the judge's house and report—once more—a failure.

The judge, however, didn't think Seikei had failed. "We suspect strongly now that Kitsune is involved. That means he is working for someone wealthy and highly placed, for no one else could afford his services. Which points, of course, to Lady Osuni." The judge paused to think, then asked, "Did the ninja see you?"

"I don't think so," said Seikei. "He was intent on following Ito. He didn't seem to be looking behind him."

"Ninjas have strong powers of awareness. But clearly Ito was his target."

"Do you think he's dead?" Seikei asked.

"Ito? Possibly. If so, you mustn't blame yourself. He chose to leave here, though he knew of the danger."

The judge looked at Seikei. "You too must be fully aware of what a serious situation this is. You defeated Kitsune once before. He is not accustomed to losing, and would welcome the chance to take revenge. On you."

"I am not afraid," said Seikei.

"Then you disappoint me, for you should be. Kitsune has many skills—all deadly. I wonder if it would not be best for you to go to Shizuoka and search for Korin, the carpenter who is one of the seven tattooed men."

"Shizuoka?" It was a small town a few days' ride from Edo. "Have you received word that Korin is there?"

"A fire recently destroyed much of the town," the judge replied. "That means there will be a great deal of work for carpenters. Several of these tattooed men seem to have adopted a rootless, wandering existence. It seems likely that Korin would be among the carpenters who will appear there in search of jobs."

Seikei could not deny the likelihood of this, but his disappointment at being sent away must have shown. The judge shook his head. "I am afraid, my son, that you have faced danger so often that you are bored when you are not risking your life."

"I will do as you wish, Father."

"Do not forget that I rely on you to say the memorial prayers for me for forty-nine days after I am dead."

Seikei was concerned. "Father, aren't you feeling well?"

The judge smiled. "Perfectly well. That is why I hope you will value your own safety a bit more."

THE CARPENTER'S SURPRISE

*T*he judge told Seikei to take along copies of the three maps they had already seen. "If you find Korin, ask him if he recognizes any of the landmarks on them. Since it seems one of the seven maps may be impossible for us to recover, we will have to do our best with those we can obtain."

By the time Seikei arose in the morning, Bunzo had already left to look for the firefighter. Noka fixed a *bento* box for Seikei to take. He knew it would contain all of his favorite foods.

Though Seikei was sixteen now, Noka still treated him as if he were a child. "Be sure to remember to eat," she told him.

"I'll bet you didn't tell Bunzo to eat when *he* left," Seikei said.

"He doesn't need to eat," Noka said. "He's big enough."

Even the judge's mind seemed to be more on food than solving the crime. "If you can, bring back some of that green tea," he said absentmindedly as Seikei was saddling his horse. Shizuoka was famous for its green tea.

Seikei rode off, starting to feel that the judge's main purpose in sending him to Shizuoka was to get him out of harm's way. Of course Korin *might* be there, but he could be in any of a thousand other places as well.

The Tokaido Road, the great highway that connected Edo, Kyoto and Osaka, was crowded as usual. No carts were permitted here, so those without horses had to carry their belongings and merchandise on their backs. Some rigged palanquins that enabled two people, or even four, to share heavy loads. But the majority shouldered boxes of tea, or bags of rice, or whatever else they hoped to sell. Others carried the tools of their trade, and there were, as the judge had guessed, many with the hammers and saws that identified them as carpenters.

From horseback, Seikei glanced down as he passed each group, looking for his only clue: the tattooed numbers ya-ku-za. One barrel-chested man attracted Seikei's attention because he was wearing gloves. Of course they were only the work gloves that many carpenters used to protect their hands. When the man noticed Seikei staring at him, he asked, "Are you in need of a carpenter, sir?"

Seikei had donned plain clothes because he didn't want to make it known that he was the son of a high official, but his hair and swords still marked him as a samurai. "No," he replied, but the man continued as if Seikei hadn't spoken: "Because I do the finest work. Careful, straight cuts. Small jobs or large. Clean, neat and honest. You won't need to hide your valuables when I'm around."

"I really don't need a carpenter," said Seikei.

"You know," the man replied, "that's when you need a carpenter most, when you don't think you do."

Seikei urged his horse forward, but though the carpenter's legs were short, he could walk fast. And talk at the same time. "The hidden leak in the roof that can cause a tremendous expense if it's not fixed soon, the termites under the floor, the loose steps that some loved one can slip on and fall . . . You have aged parents?"

Unfortunately the road was too crowded for Seikei to simply gallop off. "I'm looking for someone with numbers between his fingers," Seikei said, merely to shut the man up.

"Beg pardon?"

"Numbers tattooed between his fingers," Seikei said. "Seen anyone like that?"

The man's sudden silence was surprising enough to make Seikei look down. He saw the man appraising him carefully.

"You do know someone like that?" Seikei asked.

"Would it . . . be worth something to you if I did?" he replied, rubbing his chin.

"Well . . . yes." Seikei had never had to bribe anyone for information. He wasn't sure how much to offer. "But I'd need to *see* the person."

"Oh, you could see him. That would be no problem."

"Do you happen to know . . . if he has a large tattoo on his back?" Seikei asked.

A look of alarm momentarily passed across the man's face, and Seikei was afraid he'd said the wrong thing. "Well," the man said, "it's better not to mention that, sir. He's a bit sensitive about it."

"All right, but when can I see him?"

"Um, there was that little matter of . . ." The man winked.

"Oh, yes. I forgot. How much do you want?"

"Say five *ryo?*" the man suggested.

Seikei wasn't sure if that was too high a price, but he agreed. However, when he saw the man trying to control the smile that spread across his face, he realized it was too much. Still, it would help him carry out his assignment.

At least he knew enough to refuse to give the man the money until he actually brought Korin to Seikei. They agreed to meet that evening at a noodle shop in Shizuoka. The man, who gave his name as Bunji, told Seikei how to get there.

Shizuoka did not appear to be an exciting place. Ieyasu,

the first Tokugawa shogun, had gone to live there in his retirement. Otherwise, its importance came from its location on the Tokaido Road. Thus, many travelers stopped there for the night. Unfortunately the recent fire had destroyed many of the city's inns, and most travelers now went on to the next town on the road. It cost Seikei ten ryo in "thank money" to get even a small room in a second-class inn. This was becoming an expensive trip!

After a bath in a wooden tub of not-very-hot water, Seikei set out for the noodle shop. It was in a section of town that catered to rough-living workmen in search of entertainment. Though the sun had barely set, men who appeared to have already had too much sake staggered out of doorways. In front of other establishments, women encouraged customers to come inside for music and other pleasures. Dressed as *geishas*, these women seemed only shabby imitations to Seikei. He had known truly glamorous geishas while helping solve a case in the Yoshiwara section of Edo. Still, unlike other parts of the city, this neighborhood did a thriving business. There were many carpenters, roofers and masonry workers in the city, and few places for them to spend their wages.

The noodle shop was so crowded that Seikei could hardly squeeze through the door. Though the room held a few low tables and mats, most people simply obtained a bowl of noodles from a serving counter, and stood slurping the broth directly from the bowl.

Seikei followed suit. Though he was hungry, having finished his bento box meal on the road, he was horrified at how bad the soup was. The broth would have been better if it had been merely water. Instead it tasted like . . . Seikei couldn't actually think of anything this bad that he'd ever tasted before. And the noodles had been cooked so long that they were mushy.

He was distracted when somebody tapped him on the shoulder. He turned to find Bunji standing there. "How do you like the noodles?" he asked Seikei. "Delicious, eh?"

Seikei wondered if the man could be serious. Instead of answering, he asked, "Have you brought the man with the tattoo?"

"He wasn't hungry, so he's waiting for us outside."

Seikei thought this showed good sense if Korin had ever eaten in the noodle shop before. He set down his own bowl and motioned for Bunji to lead the way.

"Did you bring the seven ryo?" Bunji asked.

"We agreed on five ryo," Seikei replied.

"Oh, yes, I forgot," said the man, waving his hand. Seikei noticed he was still wearing his work gloves.

"I have the money," said Seikei, "but you can't have it till I see the man."

"He's in one of the geisha houses."

Seikei began to grow suspicious. "I thought you said he was outside."

Bunji smiled. "It's hard to keep him in one place. I told

you he was sensitive about his tattoo. What do you want with him anyway?"

"I'll let *him* know that when we meet," said Seikei. "Do you want the five ryo or not?"

"Sure, sure," said Bunji. "Just follow me." He started down the street. The trip was farther than Seikei expected. They went beyond the busiest area, and as Seikei looked ahead, all he could see were the remnants of some buildings that had been destroyed in the recent fire. Before he could ask where they were going, however, two men came out of an alley in front of him. Seikei reached for his sword a moment too late. Bunji had grabbed his arm, and in a flash one of the men seized the other.

"Don't let him draw the sword," the third man said. He pulled open Seikei's jacket and began to search him.

"He's got money, I know it," Bunji said to his accomplices.

Seikei struggled, but the two men who held him were stronger. Angrily, he lifted his legs to shove the third man away. "Help!" he shouted, knowing that they were probably too far from the crowds for him to be heard.

Suddenly, something swift and black sped past Seikei's head. He heard one of the men holding him cry out. A rustle of cloth preceded a cry from Bunji. Seikei felt them release his arms. In front of him, Seikei saw a look of fear cross the third man's face before he was struck down by what looked like a heavy black pole.

Without knowing what he would be fighting, Seikei started to draw his sword. Then a hand covered his own,

and a feeling of calm spread through his body. "No need for that," he heard a voice say.

Somehow, he believed it, and let his sword fall back into place. Seikei turned to see a face he had hoped never to see again. Smoothing out his black kosode was the ninja Kitsune.

10

WARN FIRST, THEN KILL

*S*eikei stammered without making sense, for he didn't know what to say. "How did you—" But then he remembered Kitsune was a master of the martial arts, and now saw him tucking away a *hana-neji,* a thick, short fighting stick. Pitting him against three carpenters wasn't fair—for the carpenters.

"Why did you—" Seikei began again. That seemed like a better question.

"Don't samurai have manners any longer?" Kitsune said. The distinctive yellow eyes flickered in Seikei's direction. "Or do you just take it as part of your due that people should save your life whenever possible?"

"I think they were only going to rob me," said Seikei.

"Oh, my mistake," said Kitsune. He nodded toward the three figures on the ground. "Shall we wake them up and let them continue?"

"No," said Seikei. "You're correct. I owe you my thanks. But why—"

"Not out of any affection, I assure you." Kitsune put his face close to Seikei's. Numerous scars bore testimony to the life Kitsune had led. "I thought I recognized you, back in Edo, when you were following the monkey man. I saw you once before, on Miwayama, didn't I?"

Seikei nodded. He might as well admit it.

"You had a *gofu* to protect you then, as I recall?"

The stone with spiritual power had been given to Seikei by Kitsune's brother, who owed Judge Ooka a favor.

"But I sense you don't have one now," Kitsune said slowly.

Seikei made no response to that.

"Nevertheless," said Kitsune, "I am a merciful person. Before I kill you, I will give you a warning."

The ninja moved another step forward. Seikei refused to retreat. He put his hand on the hilt of his sword.

"You cannot defeat me," Kitsune said.

"Then I will die in the attempt," Seikei replied.

Kitsune considered this, then shook his head. "There is no reason for us to fight at all."

"I was not threatening *you*," said Seikei.

"You are doing it without realizing it," Kitsune replied. "For example, what brings you to Shizuoka?"

"Well . . ." Seikei was certain Kitsune knew the answer, but why tell him?

"You are looking for a certain carpenter, who has a tattoo on his back," Kitsune said. "But do you see the problem that presents for me?"

"What?"

"I want that tattoo, and so you cannot have it."

"We could both have it," said Seikei.

If the ninja were capable of a smile, one might have crossed his face then. "Sharing," he said, drawing the word out so that Seikei felt foolish. "I've often had people suggest that to me. One time, a man stole a bag of coins from his employer, a powerful daimyo. The daimyo hired me to recover the money and punish the thief. He didn't care so much about the money, but the insult to his high status was insufferable. He wanted to set an example.

"The thief was not so difficult to find—for me—and when he learned what I was there for, he offered to share the loot. He was generous. Half of it would be for me. All I had to do was let him go." He looked at Seikei. "What should I have done?" he asked.

"You said you were merciful," Seikei reminded him.

Kitsune raised a finger as if scolding a pupil. "But not foolish. Why let him have half when I could take all? Which I did, of course. You see, when people offer to share, I take it as a sign of weakness. I never share. I don't have to. I brought the thief's head to the daimyo and told him the man had spent the money. The daimyo was pleased, as I knew he would be. None of his servants ever stole from him again."

Seikei swallowed hard and said, "But this is a different situation."

"Oh, it's very similar, I assure you. My employer wants the maps only for herself. She doesn't wish to share." He cocked his head sideways. "But perhaps you have some maps you wish to share with me? How many? Did you get the one from the monkey man?"

"Did you kill him?" Seikei asked.

Kitsune waved away the question. "That is water under the bridge, if you catch my *drift*."

"You didn't have to kill him."

"That was part of the agreement he made."

"What agreement?"

"He, along with the others, was paid to carry a map on his back. They all knew that someday they would be required to give up the map. Now, wouldn't you know, they're making it difficult. That's why I was brought in."

"Was it you who stripped the skin from the man who was attacked in the rice field?"

"Are you looking for me to confess to crimes again? Because I am well aware of who your father is."

"Why not just draw a copy of the map? Why take the skin?"

"Is that what you're doing? Drawing? How many do you have?"

"Enough," said Seikei.

Kitsune sneered. "Who are you trying to fool? I'm in-

sulted now, I really am. In the first place, you waste time making drawings. If someone is running away from you, which is more efficient, drawing him or killing him? Second, the drawings may not be accurate. How do you know what's important and what is only a mole, a scar, a mosquito bite? I'll wager you don't even know where the place is that's on these maps."

He eyed Seikei, who realized he was being tested and tried to appear knowledgeable.

"Finally," Kitsune continued, "you cannot possibly assemble all the maps. I have good reason to know. Once I have a map, it can never be yours. So your task is hopeless." His yellow eyes blazed like lanterns. "Go home. Play with your toys. Stay out of my way. That is your warning."

He looked down. "And you'd better start now, because your friends are starting to come to."

It was true. The three thieves were moaning softly. "I don't think they'll put up a fight," Seikei said. But he realized he was talking to the air. Kitsune had dissolved into the night, and Seikei knew it was useless to try to follow him. He drew his short sword, which was sharp enough to frighten the trio.

"I could kill you if I wished," Seikei told Bunji and his accomplices. They knew he spoke the truth. Any samurai could take the life of a common workman. The fact that they had attacked him was reason enough to do so. They sat rubbing their heads and looking warily at Seikei.

"Tell me one thing and I may be merciful to you," Seikei said, hoping he sounded as menacing as Kitsune.

"What is that?" asked Bunji.

"Tell him anything he wants, you fool," said one of his friends.

That was what Seikei was afraid of—that they would tell any lie to get him to let them go free.

"I want to know where to find the carpenter with the tattoo on his back."

Bunji didn't reply. Seikei saw the calculating look on his face again. Whether he was figuring out a convincing lie or wondering if he should betray the man with the tattoo, Seikei didn't know.

The friend started to speak. "He's—" But Bunji interrupted.

"He'll be helping to rebuild the Rinzaiji Temple," Bunji said. The other two man looked at each other, making Seikei suspicious.

"All right," said Seikei. "Now get up. I'm going to take you to the local magistrate."

"What?" the other man exclaimed. "You said you would let us go."

"I said I would be merciful," Seikei replied. "The magistrate will detain you for only a day or two. I can't have you warning this man that I'm looking for him."

"He already—" the other man began, but Bunji hushed him with a wave of his gloved hand. That was bad, Seikei thought, because it meant his quarry would be on guard.

The trio continued to protest, but Seikei had the sword, and they obeyed.

When they reached the local magistrate's headquarters, it turned out that the man knew Judge Ooka, and was cooperative. "I can hold them as long as you wish," he told Seikei.

"A couple of days should be fine for my purpose," Seikei told him. "But they're thieves."

"I'll make sure they leave town when they are released," said the magistrate.

Seikei accepted the magistrate's offer of a room for the night and in the morning set out for the Rinzaiji Temple. In this part of town, the fire had burned most fiercely, and whole blocks of buildings were nothing but flat, charred ruins. When he approached the temple, however, he saw that some of the structures were still standing.

Seikei saw that the repair work was in its earliest stages. Large logs, whose bark had been stripped, were being carefully sawed into planks. One end of a log was propped into the air on a scaffold. Men scrambled to the top, using large handsaws to cut through the length of the trunk. It was hard, hot work and the men had stripped to their loincloths so they wouldn't soil their clothing with sweat. If any of them had a large tattoo on his back, he would have been easy to see—but none did. Seikei moved on to another part of the temple grounds.

A young monk, head shaved and wearing a saffron robe, approached him. "Unfortunately, the temple is closed while repairs are being made," he said.

"I am looking for a carpenter," said Seikei.

"There are many here and throughout the city," replied the monk.

"This one has an elaborate tattoo on his back."

The monk raised his eyebrows.

"You have seen someone like that?" Seikei asked.

"No, but someone else was here earlier, also looking for such a person."

"A man with yellow eyes?"

"Ah, you know him then," the monk said, nodding. "Perhaps he is a friend of yours?"

"He is a friend of no one's," said Seikei. "What did you tell him?"

"He went to make a donation to Marishi-ten. After that he may have found an answer."

Seikei realized that the monk was hinting that he too should make a donation. "Marishi-ten is the patroness of all warriors, isn't she?" he asked the monk.

"Indeed so, and the image of her that is honored here brought success to Ieyasu, the ancestor of our present shogun. During Ieyasu's struggle to defeat his enemies, he carried this image with his army."

Seikei remembered hearing the story. "Will Marishi-ten help me?"

"She helps all who revere her. She shines her light in the eyes of their enemies. Blinded, they cannot see where Marishi-ten's friends are going."

Seikei thought he understood. "If I make a donation, will I see where the yellow-eyed man has gone?"

"I would not delay, if I were you," said the monk.

11 —
MESSAGE AT THE TEMPLE

*T*he statue of Marishi-ten was in a separate building that the fire had not damaged. To prevent the blaze from reaching it, the monks had carried water in baskets and doused any sparks that landed on the roof. As a result, the interior of the shrine had a musty smell.

Candles—dozens of them—surrounded the statue, throwing flickering shadows on the tall, multicolored figure. As Seikei approached, he saw that the goddess actually had three heads, as well as six arms, each of which held a weapon.

It was impressive and a little frightening to look up at Marishi-ten's fierce visages. He realized that each face represented a different aspect of the true warrior. One face was wide-eyed and ferocious: courage. Another was composed and peaceful: the serenity that comes from the acceptance of life and death as part of an endless cycle. The third was

more puzzling. It had a face that amazingly resembled a pig. Seikei noticed now that Marishi-ten actually stood on a cart that was drawn by a team of pigs.

Mysterious, as were many things in Buddhist temples. Seikei waited for enlightenment. He knew that Kitsune had been here and received some kind of answer by making an offering. Seikei took a five-ryo coin and placed it in the basket that sat before the statues. Five ryo had been enough to tempt Bunji and his friends to rob Seikei. Maybe it would bring a better result this time.

He knelt before the image, trying to clear his mind so that an answer could come to him. Irritatingly, the image of the pig's head filled his mind as other thoughts departed. Seikei couldn't do anything about it: the pig ran free of its own accord.

The pig must be the side of every person that acted without thinking, like an animal. The judge had once told Seikei that everyone was capable of committing a crime. "If you do not recognize that you have a part of yourself that could commit crimes, then you may not be alert enough to stop yourself when the temptation comes," said the judge. The image of Marishi-ten was a reminder of that.

Discovering the meaning of the pig's head allowed Seikei to dismiss it from his mind. Suspended like an insect floating on the surface of a fog-shrouded pond, he waited now for the answer he was seeking.

Gloves.

The man who called himself Bunji wore gloves—even when he came to meet Seikei at the noodle house. Even when his intention was to rob Seikei.

He didn't need gloves for that.

Seikei rose to his feet and mentally thanked Marishiten. Trying not to run, he left the shrine, but the monk, waiting outside, saw his eagerness.

"Did you find the answer you were seeking?" he asked.

"It was there all along, but I didn't realize it," Seikei responded.

The monk nodded as if he understood perfectly. Seikei turned to go, but remembered something else he wanted to ask: "Did . . . did the man with yellow eyes find the answer he was seeking?"

"I cannot say," the monk replied, "but he seemed to have purpose and direction when he left."

Seikei hoped that Kitsune did not know Bunji was in jail. Though jail might seem a safe place to be, Seikei was sure that Kitsune was perfectly capable of getting in—or out, for that matter.

Fortunately, when Seikei arrived, the magistrate reported that Bunji was still in a locked cell. A samurai guard showed Seikei to it and let him inside.

Bunji stood up and smiled. "I'm glad you came back, sir," he said. "I hope you'll allow me to explain about the misunderstanding."

"The misunderstanding," Seikei said, "is that I thought you and your friends were trying to rob me."

"No, we thought you were trying to rob *us,* you see, and—"

"I don't want to hear it," Seikei said. "I know who you are." He looked down at Bunji's hands. The man was still wearing gloves. Seikei didn't need to see his fingers.

"Take off your kosode," Seikei said. "I want to see your back."

Bunji took a step backward, leaning against the wall. "Why would you want me to do such a thing?" he asked.

Seikei ignored him. "I can bring guards here to hold you down if I have to."

Bunji tried to bluff it out. "I'm not who you think I am. You've made a mistake."

"Your real name is Korin, and you have a tattoo on your back. You should be glad I've found you. There's someone else searching for you who will slice the skin off and take it. I can get what I need just by making a copy."

Bunji shook his head. "She told us if we ever let someone do that, she would kill us anyway."

"Who?" Seikei already knew, but wanted Bunji to confirm it.

"I can't tell you."

"Lady Osuni?"

Bunji's eyes widened. "I never told you that."

"You have nothing to be afraid of," Seikei said. "I will make sure—"

Without warning, Bunji let out a cry and rushed across the cell, trying to grab one of Seikei's swords.

Seikei sidestepped the man, took him by the arm and slammed him headfirst against a wooden post. It was a maneuver Bunzo had taught him, but Seikei had never used it before. He was a little surprised it had worked so well. The man lay on the floor, dazed.

Seikei called the guard, and they dragged Bunji into a room where there was better light. In the end, two guards had to hold down Bunji—or Korin, for it really was him—while Seikei copied the tattoo.

The guards were puzzled that Korin was putting up so much of a fight. "He's not going to hurt you," one of them told him. "He's only drawing a picture."

When Seikei finished, he went to the magistrate's office. "You'll have to keep the prisoner longer than I thought," Seikei said.

"What's he done now?"

"Nothing more than before, but someone will try to capture him."

The magistrate gave Seikei a skeptical look. "Why would anyone want to capture him? He's already in jail."

"I don't mean the shogun's officials," said Seikei. "Someone . . . someone else."

The magistrate shrugged and said, "We'll keep him for a while, but this is not an inn. We'll have to feed him, assign a guard to look in on him . . ."

"He should be guarded at all times," said Seikei.

The magistrate shook his head. "Impossible. Frankly, it is my understanding that you have already made a copy of this map on his back."

"That's right."

"So you are finished with him."

"But the idea is to keep anyone *else* from getting the map," Seikei said.

"I see," said the magistrate, but Seikei realized that he didn't.

It couldn't be helped. He had to get back to Edo and tell the judge he had found another map. Even more important, perhaps, the judge must be told about Kitsune. The fact that the ninja wanted the maps made the task of collecting them even more urgent.

But as Seikei walked to the stables to get his horse, Bunzo came riding up.

"I thought I'd find you near the magistrate's headquarters," the judge's assistant said. "Did you get yourself tossed in jail again?"

Seikei felt his face redden. "That happened only once," he said.

"Never happened to *me*," Bunzo growled. "Anyway, we found the firefighter with a tattoo on his back. The judge wanted to know if you stumbled across the carpenter."

"Actually, I did," said Seikei. "He's in the jail here."

"You made a copy of his tattoo?"

"Yes."

"Has the magistrate released him?"

"No." Seikei explained about Kitsune. "We've got to keep him from capturing the carpenter."

"We can do better than that," said Bunzo. "You're sure Kitsune will try to take the carpenter from the jail?"

"Yes."

"Then we'll be waiting, and turn the tables on him."

"How?"

"We'll capture Kitsune. Lady Osuni won't be able to carry out her scheme without him."

Seikei drew a sharp breath. Could even Bunzo do that?

12 —
OVERCONFIDENCE

*I*t was a new experience for Seikei to share a cell with Bunzo. They occupied the one next to the carpenter's. As soon as Kitsune made his move, Bunzo and Seikei would trap him.

At least, that was the plan. Although Seikei couldn't exactly see any flaw in it, he felt they were underestimating Kitsune. "I saw him defeat three men before they even realized they were being attacked," Seikei warned Bunzo. "And he was only using his hands and a fighting stick."

"They were carpenters," replied Bunzo. "You could probably have defeated them yourself if you'd been more alert."

Seikei had to admit he'd been off guard. "But Kitsune has many weapons. And he can change into the form of a fox."

"If he's a fox, he can't drag our prisoner very far," Bunzo said. "You know what Kitsune's greatest weakness is?"

Seikei was curious. As far as he knew, Kitsune had no weaknesses.

"His overconfidence," Bunzo declared. "He's so used to people fearing him because he knows a few tricks and sneaks around in the middle of the night that he thinks he cannot be defeated. I'm surprised that you believe it. Remember when you marched onto his sacred mountain and forced him to confess to a murder?"

Seikei could hardly have forgotten. It was one of his proudest moments. He had been given his two swords in recognition. "But when that happened," he reminded Bunzo, "I had a gofu, a stone that contained a spirit. I traded it for the confession."

Bunzo shrugged. "I have something better than a magic rock." He patted the two hilts at his *obi*. "I have my swords."

Seikei's spine tingled. He'd seen Bunzo practicing with wooden swords, which he wielded so swiftly that the air whistled. As for his real swords, Seikei had seen Bunzo unsheathe them to polish and sharpen them. Only once had he seen Bunzo use them. To test the long blade's sharpness, Bunzo had taken Seikei to the execution grounds. There the dead bodies of criminals were displayed as a warning to those tempted to violate the law.

Bunzo had found a body that was relatively fresh and suspended it from a rope. With one blow of his sword, he had sliced it in two. Witnessing that, Seikei felt a mixture of awe and fear that anyone could wield such power. The same emotions swept through him now as he won-

dered how he would feel if Bunzo did the same thing to Kitsune.

Time passed. Seikei could hear snores coming from the cell next door. They had not wanted to alarm the carpenter by telling him they were there for his protection. Seikei himself felt weary, but he was too nervous to sleep. Across the cell, he knew Bunzo sat as alert as a cat—breathing softly, ready to spring into action. That thought alone was enough to prevent Seikei from falling asleep.

Seikei remembered Kitsune's warning that Seikei could not defeat him. "Then I will die in the attempt," Seikei had told the ninja.

Were those only words? Or did they have a meaning? Seikei reminded himself, as he often did, that a samurai faced the truth that others shrank from: that someday he must die. And so, why not die bravely, with honor, instead of crawling on your belly to extend life a little longer?

He knew that Bunzo didn't need to ask himself such questions, and that made it a little easier for Seikei to sit here, waiting for death.

Gradually he became aware of another sound, just a little less loud than the snoring. It sounded like scratching. A mouse chewing through one of the pine walls?

He sniffed the air. Very faintly, he detected smoke. He started to warn Bunzo, but the giant samurai was already on his feet. Noiselessly, he opened the cell door. Seikei rose and stood behind him. There was no doubt that the smell was stronger here.

No one else had noticed, for the snoring in the other cells continued peacefully. Seikei felt Bunzo press something into his hand: the key that would unlock the carpenter's cell. "Get him out of the way," Bunzo whispered. "I'm going after the ninja."

He headed for the doorway, not waiting for questions. Seikei unlocked the cell door and found the carpenter asleep on a mat. He shook the man roughly. "Hurry up," he said frantically. "We've got to get out of here." The smoke was starting to seep in through chinks in the wooden wall. It was there, outside the jail, that Kitsune was setting a fire.

Korin, the carpenter, misunderstood what Seikei was trying to do. "No!" he cried, rolling across the floor. "I'm not going! Help!" he screamed. "Where are the guards?"

He had moved just in time, for at that moment the wall next to his sleeping mat burst into flames. The ninja must have used something to make it burn quickly.

"I'm trying to *save* you!" Seikei shouted at the carpenter. "Come with me. Now!"

The man stared at the flames, his face torn with uncertainty. Then he realized there was only one way out. He looked at Seikei and nodded.

Seikei led him into the hallway. Other guards were awake now, unlocking cell doors. People were shouting. It was impossible to hear what might be going on outside. Seikei wanted to go and help Bunzo, but his duty was to keep the carpenter safe. He grasped the man's arm and pulled him

toward the other side of the building. Men ran past them carrying buckets of water. With any luck they would be able to extinguish the fire before it spread. Seikei knew it would be a mistake to bring the carpenter outside: that was what Kitsune was hoping for. Out in the open he could capture the carpenter as he had the monkey-keeper.

But the carpenter had other ideas. "Where are you taking me?" he asked.

"Where you'll be safe," said Seikei.

"The building is on fire! We've got to get out!"

"You'll be protected here," Seikei reassured him.

"No!" With a lunge, the man broke free and began to run in the other direction.

Seikei followed, but by now the building was filling with smoke. He breathed in some of it and began to cough.

Stumbling forward, he reached the entrance to the cells. Surely the carpenter would have turned toward the outer entrance here. Seikei went in that direction and found his way blocked by a crowd of prisoners who had been assembled there to save them from the fire. Seikei saw one of the two men who had helped Korin attack him. "Have you seen Kor—, I mean Bunji?" he asked the man, who gave him a suspicious look.

"He was running away from somebody," the man said.

"He doesn't understand," Seikei protested. "I'm trying to save him."

The man shrugged and pointed toward the front of the building.

Seikei pushed his way through the crowd and found his way to the entrance, which was guarded by two samurai. "Did anyone come through here?" he asked them.

"A samurai brought a prisoner out," one of them replied.

"A samurai? What did he look like?"

The two guards looked at each other, puzzled. "Did you get a good look at him?" one of them asked.

"I can't recall," the other responded.

It must have been Kitsune, Seikei thought. That was one of the ninja skills—to pass by people unnoticed. "How about the prisoner?" he asked. "Did you see *him*?"

"Oh, yes," said one of the guards. "Top-heavy man. Big chest, short legs. About thirty years old. Looked harmless."

Seikei's heart sank. A perfect description of Korin. Kitsune must have caught him after all. But then . . . what had happened to Bunzo?

Alarmed, Seikei rushed outside and ran around the side of the building. Firefighters had already arrived and were climbing ladders, pulling burning pieces of the roof off. Others brought buckets of water, keeping the fire confined to one section of the wall.

Seikei found his path blocked by a burly firefighter. "You can't go back there," the man said.

"I must," Seikei responded. "I'm looking for a samurai who may be—" Loyalty to Bunzo made him unwilling to finish the sentence. Bunzo couldn't be wounded or dead. That was impossible. But then, why had the ninja escaped

from his trap? "He's . . . having trouble," Seikei finally explained.

"Everyone back there is having trouble," the firefighter told him. "The air is filled with poison. If you breathe it, you get sick. Who knows? Maybe die. I dragged two men away from it after they passed out. There may be more back there."

"Then I *must* see if my friend is there," Seikei said. He touched the hilt of his sword.

The firefighter, who was not a samurai, shrugged. "I warned you," he said, and turned his back.

Seikei took a deep breath and rushed forward. If the air was bad, then he would just have to force himself not to breathe.

13 —
"I CAN TELL WHEN PEOPLE ARE LYING"

*T*he flames were still licking away at the rear of the building. They made it easier to see, and as soon as Seikei rounded the corner, he spotted a body on the ground. His heart leaped.

A moment later he realized it was a firefighter, not Bunzo. The man had carried a pail of water, which rested on the ground beside him, still full. He evidently had collapsed slowly, almost as if he had fallen asleep.

Seikei moved on. It was becoming more difficult to hold his breath. Then he saw what he most feared: Bunzo, lying near the spot where the fire had apparently begun. Next to him, planted firmly in the earth, was a large incense stick. At least that was what it resembled: the tip gave off a thin trail of smoke as it burned without a flame.

Realizing it must be the source of the poisonous air, Seikei ran back to the side of the building. He fell to his knees and drew in lungfuls of fresh air. He feared he

wasn't far enough away, but he had to breathe. After a moment, he felt slightly dizzy, but not as if he were going to pass out.

He told himself to think clearly. Bunzo and the firefighter only appeared to be sleeping, but what if they continued to breathe the poisonous air? Seikei realized what he had to do. He ran back to the firefighter and picked up the bucket of water. It was heavy. Firefighters built up the muscles in their arms through constant practice and exercise. Seikei had to half-carry, half-drag the bucket to where Bunzo lay. There he yanked the burning stick from the ground and plunged it into the bucket of water. He heard a low hissing sound.

Still trying not to breathe, he ran back a safe distance again. He didn't know how long it would take the poisonous air to disappear, but after a few anxious moments he saw Bunzo begin to stir.

Seikei ran to his side. "Bunzo!" he cried. "Are you all right?"

Bunzo shook his head. "Get away from here," he said weakly. "There's something wrong with the air."

"No, I fixed that." Quickly, Seikei explained.

After a while Bunzo got up, rubbing his head. "What happened to the prisoner?" he asked.

Seikei hung his head. "I lost him," he admitted. "Kitsune must have him. I'm sorry."

"Not your fault," said Bunzo. "I was the one who was

overconfident, not him. I ran back here expecting to fight him. I didn't even see him—nothing here but a burning stick."

"He didn't defeat you in a fair fight," Seikei said. "It was a trick."

"But we knew ninjas have plenty of those, didn't we?" said Bunzo. "Next time . . ." He didn't finish his thought. "For now, we must return to Edo and tell the judge we have failed."

When they arrived, the judge saw by the looks on their faces what had happened. He listened to the story without comment, but then said, "You succeeded in the most important thing."

"What was that?" said Seikei. He *had* remembered to buy green tea before leaving Shizuoka. Perhaps the judge regarded that as the most vital part of his mission.

"You have brought back a copy of the map," the judge said.

"Well, yes," Seikei said, "but Kitsune has that map too. We wanted to keep it away from him."

"A pity, yes, but we have learned a bit more about Kitsune," said the judge.

"He said that if he had taken a map, it could never be mine."

"Apparently because he removes the skin that holds the map," said the judge. "A sloppy procedure, I might add. It

was correct of you to think you should keep the carpenter away from Kitsune. Too bad the carpenter didn't see the wisdom of it."

"Why didn't he tell me who he was in the first place?" Seikei asked.

"Fear," said the judge. "The men who carry these maps have an idea what fate has in store for them. When they allowed themselves to be tattooed, they saw only the money that was promised. They didn't understand that the path shown on their backs would one day lead to death."

"And now they do," Seikei said. "But what about Boko, the first one to die? We don't have his map, and can't get it."

"A difficulty, to be sure," the judge said. "But we have two maps that Kitsune does not have."

Seikei was surprised, but then began to think about it. "The firefighter," he said. "Bunzo told me you found him."

"Yes. He's here in my house. In a little while you will copy his map."

"Who is the other? Did you find the gambler too?"

"Not yet. But while you and Bunzo were gone, I did a little work myself." He smiled. "Not physical work, to be sure. But I sent two trusted men to a place you and Bunzo had visited before."

"Where was that?"

"The hiding place of the thief named Rofu. And look what they returned with." The judge tapped a small gong, and two samurai entered the room, holding a chastened

Rofu between them. When he looked up and saw Seikei, his knees buckled.

"Let him go," said the judge. "I think he understands that he cannot escape."

Rofu fell to his knees and then prostrated himself in front of the judge.

"Rofu," said the judge, "I believe my son told you I would like to ask you some questions."

A muffled sound came from the floor.

"Come, come, Rofu, sit up so we can hear you," said the judge.

Slowly Rofu rose, but he remained kneeling. His eyes flicked around the room, noticing everything, including Bunzo and the guards. Though he tried to appear as humble as possible, it was clear he was calculating what story would be most likely to get him out of trouble.

"Rofu," the judge said in a tone that immediately brought Rofu's eyes to him. "I want you to know something."

"Yes, your honor," Rofu said, all attention and respect.

"I can tell when people are lying to me."

Rofu nodded and attempted to smile. The expression on his face was more like that of a person suffering from gas. Seikei had to carefully hide his own smile. The judge had told him people were more likely to betray themselves if they thought he could detect their lies.

Once, when the judge was a young man, he had to discover who had stolen some money that an old woman had hidden inside a pickle jar. The household had many ser-

vants, but all denied being the guilty party. The judge had gathered them together and announced that he intended to smell their hands since the thief had dipped his fingers into the pickle brine.

"Now, the theft had taken place two days earlier," the judge had told Seikei. "So the odor of pickles would probably have faded. But I watched carefully as I made my announcement, and one man in the back lifted his hand to smell his fingers. That was the thief. Knowing that made it easy to get him to confess."

In the same way, now that Rofu believed the judge could tell when he was lying, he would be much more nervous if he tried to lie.

"Let us begin again," said the judge. "You *do* remember that my son said I would like to ask you some questions?"

"Yes," admitted Rofu.

"Then why did you hide when my assistant Bunzo came to visit?"

Rofu looked at Bunzo. "Is that who—I mean . . ."

"Bunzo found some things in your hiding place under the street," the judge continued. He motioned for Bunzo to display them. Rofu's mouth twitched as Bunzo brought out the two Buddhist figurines and the chest of silk kimonos.

"Merchandise," Rofu said finally. "I am a merchant."

"Where did you obtain this merchandise?" the judge asked.

Rofu waved his hands vaguely. "People bring these

things to me. I pay for them. I paid for everything you have there."

"Would it surprise you to learn that any of these items had been stolen?"

Rofu licked his lips. "If they are, I had no knowledge of it. A merchant must deal with the people who come to him to buy and sell."

"Even if the merchant lives in a hole in the ground," the judge added dryly. "Why do you have such an unusual place of business?"

"I find it safer there," Rofu replied.

"I have one other item that Bunzo found," the judge said. He held up the gold bracelet set with glittering gems, which Bunzo had thought too expensive for a petty thief to possess.

Rofu's face paled, and he started to reach for the bracelet before he caught himself. "That's . . ." he began to say, but changed his mind and said, "You must be mistaken. I've never seen that bracelet before."

The judge sighed. "Didn't I say I could tell when you were lying?" Seikei smiled, for even *he* could tell this was a lie.

But Rofu was stubborn. "Anyone could have left it there."

Seikei thought the judge would press him further. Instead, he took another path entirely.

"The tattoo on your back . . . You allowed my son to copy it, when you could easily have gotten away. Why was that?"

"What harm was there in that?" Rofu's smile was very weak now. "He said you wanted a copy. I always cooperate with the shogun's officials when I can."

The judge shook his head. "You said you had a reason. I believe the reason was that you intended to put him in danger."

Rofu's hands began to tremble. He realized it, and put them flat on the floor so they wouldn't move. "I would never do that, your honor," he said.

"No?" the judge said. "Suppose I just let you go now, and allow you to walk home?"

Seikei looked at the judge to see if he was joking. But he appeared sincere. However, the offer had the opposite effect from what Seikei expected. Rofu lay flat on the floor again, pleading, "Sir, your honor, I beg you, don't do that to me."

14 —
THE SCARRED MAN

W hat are you afraid of?" the judge asked Rofu. "No one
here has harmed you. I have not even threatened to torture you, which as you know I very well could. Yet you seem
fearful when all I offered to do was set you free."

"You know why," Rofu said after a pause.

"Well, if I already know why," said the judge, "then there
is no reason for you not to tell me. Come, look at me so we
can speak."

Rofu sat up again, but looked nervously at Seikei, not
the judge. "Nothing happened to him, so it's all right,"
Rofu said. Seikei realized Rofu meant *him*.

"No, he is safe," said the judge. "But when you sent him
outside your hiding place, you thought a ninja might attack him, didn't you?"

"No, I swear I didn't. You see, if he—your son—had a
copy of the map, then the ninja would only have to take it
from him. No reason to hurt him at all."

"Whereas if the ninja took it from you . . ." the judge began.

". . . he would kill me," Rofu said with a shudder.

"Of course, he might just as easily have killed my son," the judge pointed out.

Rofu had no answer for this. Seikei remembered Kitsune saying that copies of the maps were not what he was seeking. Fortunately for Seikei.

"So you were, at least, certain that a ninja was nearby," the judge said.

"I had heard he was . . . collecting the maps," said Rofu.

"Is that how you got the bracelet?" the judge asked.

The question startled Rofu. He couldn't hide it.

The judge picked up the bracelet and displayed it. "The jewels on the side form the shapes of irises," he said. "The iris is part of the family crest of Lady Osuni. Did you obtain it from her? Shall I ask her if it was stolen?"

Rofu swallowed hard. Seikei could see him thinking again.

"No lies, Rofu," the judge snapped.

"It . . . it wasn't stolen," Rofu said.

"How then did you—"

"She sent it to me," Rofu said.

"Is that so? A lavish gift for one of Japan's richest women to present to a man who lives in a hole in the ground."

"She wanted something from me in return," Rofu said.

"It must have been important to her."

"It was."

Silence fell as the judge waited for a fuller answer. At last he said, "It is important to me as well, Rofu. But I have no gifts to offer you—except your life."

Rofu nodded. He understood. "She wanted me to tell her how to find some of the others who carried the maps."

The judge nodded, and Seikei remembered that Ito had said Rofu had suggested they all keep in touch. Rofu was selling that information to Lady Osuni.

"I kept track of them, or tried to," Rofu said. "In my business, I have friends in many places who keep me informed."

"Your business as a thief and dealer in stolen goods."

Rofu spread his hands. "Everyone has to earn a living," he said.

"Yes," replied the judge. "Now let us see if we can combine our information." He signaled to Bunzo, who left the room and soon brought back a man as large as he was. This man, however, had terrible scars on his face and arms.

Rofu gasped when he saw the man, who looked at him and nodded. "I thought you were dead, Rofu," he said calmly.

"Michio, I was only buried, not dead," Rofu replied.

"I see introductions are not necessary," said the judge. "Have you been comfortable here, Michio?"

"Yes, your honor, but I'd rather be with my comrades fighting fires," Michio replied.

"If we are successful, you may do just that," said the judge. "Would you please show us your back now?"

Michio tried to hide a smile as he turned and removed his kimono. Of all the men whose tattoos Seikei had seen, Michio had been the most successful in concealing his. Countless fires had scarred his skin, leaving a network of welts and old burns that made the map almost invisible.

"You haven't taken good care of your map, Michio," the judge commented.

"Didn't think it was likely to take care of me," the firefighter replied. "I was sorry that I ever let them put it on me. It was like becoming someone's servant for life."

The judge set Seikei to work, making as clear a copy of the map as possible. When he finished, the judge had him spread all the maps out flat on a low table. "Rofu," he said, "what can you tell us?"

"Well," Rofu replied, "three of them fit together." He arranged the maps so that the edges lined up. "Like this." He pointed to the one from his own flesh, which didn't fit with the other three. "I have been told that this is the second-to-last of the series." He picked up the one that had been on Korin's back. "Was part of this blue?" he asked Seikei.

"Yes," Seikei replied.

"It must be the first map in the series, for that should be the seacoast."

The judge pointed to some unusual marks that appeared on all five maps. "What are these supposed to represent?" he asked.

Rofu hesitated. "I was told that they are soldiers guarding the path."

The judge's eyebrows went up. "Soldiers who never move?"

"I have not seen them," said Rofu. "I only know what I was told."

"Were you told the location of the place shown on the maps?"

Rofu shook his head. "I always assumed it was within the Osuni family domain. But that is a vast territory."

"Along the seacoast at the western end of Honshu," the judge said. "Far from here. And I understand there were seven maps."

Rofu nodded.

"One of the remaining two maps is said to have been on the back of a man who is now dead."

"You've heard about Boko, then," said Rofu. "So you know you can never assemble all the maps."

"I also know," said the judge, "that as long as I can keep you and Michio safe from the ninja that he cannot possess all the maps either."

A silence fell. The judge seemed to be waiting for Rofu to reply. Yet Rofu only twitched nervously and looked miserable.

"Don't you trust me to do that?" asked the judge.

"You don't know this ninja," said Rofu.

"Actually, I do," replied the judge. "Perhaps it will sur-

prise you to learn that my son defeated him. He forced Kitsune to tell us who hired him to commit a murder."

Rofu stared at Seikei. "Where was this?" he asked.

"On Miwayama," said Seikei. "The mountain at the O-Miwa shrine."

"That's impossible," said Rofu. "If you had been underground—perhaps. Even so . . ."

"Why do you say that?" asked Seikei.

"Because you're barely more than a boy. Even a samurai like him"—his eyes went to Bunzo—"would never be able to defeat him."

"No, I meant why do you think it would have been possible if I had been underground?"

Rofu made a gesture with his hand as if to say the answer was obvious. "His power comes from the kami of the mountain, its spirit. That is why he must return to it once a year, at least. And it was also why I was safe from him underground."

The judge nodded. "You believe his power is weakened there."

"I *know* it," Rofu insisted. "Why do you think he couldn't come after me?"

"Then you should be perfectly safe in the cellar of my house," said the judge.

Michio, who had been silent till now, shook his head. "I don't want to stay in a cellar for the rest of my life, like a mushroom. I'd rather take my chances fighting fires."

"It will not be long," the judge said. "Rofu, you have no objection?"

Rofu sighed. "It is my only chance."

"Then I need only one other thing from you. Tell us where the seventh man, Gaho the gambler, is."

"He wanders up and down the Tokaido Road. Occasionally someone will tell me that they saw him in one or another of the station towns. But I learned recently he was on his way to Edo."

"How recently?"

Rofu looked uncomfortable. "Eight days ago he was dealing cards in Yoshiwara."

"And does Lady Osuni have that information?"

Rofu hung his head. "Yes."

15 —
FEEDING THE FISH

I think it is time we paid a visit to Lady Osuni," the judge said after Rofu and Michio had been taken downstairs.

"Are you going to arrest her?" asked Seikei.

"I have no proof that she has done anything wrong," said the judge.

"Well, Rofu said she gave him the bracelet to learn where the other men with maps are. And several of them have been murdered."

"Even if we accept Rofu's word—and he is obviously an untrustworthy thief who betrayed his friends—it does not prove she is responsible for killing those men."

"Do we have to get Kitsune to confess again?"

The judge smiled. "Are you confident you could do that a second time? Once proved you were brave. Twice might show you are foolhardy."

"What can we do, then?"

"You are impatient," the judge commented. "Therefore, you think we must take action."

Seikei bit his tongue. That was exactly the way he felt. Only, unlike the judge, he didn't see anything wrong with taking action. He reminded himself to listen respectfully and hope the judge would explain.

"If the ninja has already gone after Gaho the gambler," the judge said, "it is too late for us to catch up to him. What we must do is to convince Lady Osuni that *she* must take action. She may not yet be fully prepared to do so, but we will be."

Seikei saw the wisdom in this, but it was difficult to wait when the ninja might already be acting. Before leaving, the judge told Bunzo to place samurai at all entrances to the house. "Keep Michio and Rofu below ground," the judge said.

"I will stay with them myself," Bunzo responded. Bunzo had never spoken to Seikei about what had happened at the jail in Shizuoka, but Seikei knew it bothered him. Bunzo was determined to defeat the ninja if they met again—or die in the attempt.

Lady Osuni lived in a large mansion near Edo Castle. "Her estate was a gift from the shogun," the judge told Seikei.

"I thought he didn't trust her."

"That's why he wants her to live where he can keep an eye on her."

At the gate, two guards noted the hollyhock crest on the judge's clothing. They sent word inside that Lady Osuni had visitors from the shogun. The guards didn't seem to show proper respect, Seikei felt. But he knew that the judge wouldn't take offense. Or at least he wouldn't *show* he was offended. He would merely work all the harder to prove Lady Osuni was a criminal.

At last a servant came to escort them inside, leading through a series of many rooms. The rooms appeared to be simple and sparsely furnished, until Seikei looked closely at what was there. A scroll hanging on a wall bore the calligraphy of a great poet. When Seikei recognized it, he stopped to stare. It was the work of Fujiwara Teika, who had lived five hundred years earlier. The only other place Seikei had seen an example of his writing was in the shogun's castle.

Room after room held subtle treasures. A vase with an arrangement of flowers that was so carefully done it must have taken hours to prepare. A piece of pottery shaped and finished so that it resembled a natural object. Silk wall hangings, color prints, carvings . . . Seikei wished he could take time to look at each one. But the servant moved too swiftly for him to pause long.

The room where Lady Osuni awaited them was unusually bright. Seikei saw that part of the ceiling was covered by rice paper that let in sunlight. Nearly half the room had a bare stone floor that held a shallow tile pool. Lady Osuni, a slight woman with a face lined by age, sat sideways

on the edge of it, her knees folded and her feet tucked under a yellow silk kimono.

She was feeding *koi*, fish colored gold and white, who swam over to take crumbs from her hand. Apparently she could tell them apart, for she called each fish by its name.

She didn't look up as the judge and Seikei entered the room. When the servant went to her, knelt and quietly announced their arrival, she merely nodded. Only after finishing with the fish and brushing her hands together over the pool did she turn to look at the judge. She ignored Seikei altogether, which gave him a chance to study her.

Her face was made up in an old-fashioned style: eyebrows shaved and new ones drawn high on her forehead, where her hairline was shaved. White powder covered most of her face and neck so thickly that it nearly filled in the many lines, making it look smoother than it actually was.

The judge bowed politely, introducing himself and Seikei.

"I know your reputation," Lady Osuni said. "You may sit."

The judge took the largest cushion, settling himself slowly, and Seikei took a seat on a mat nearby.

"Aren't you supposed to be investigating crimes?" Lady Osuni said.

"Murder is a crime," responded the judge. "I happened to be in Echigo province when a man was attacked a few days ago."

"Is that so?" she asked. "You must be quite busy if you look into such things anywhere in Japan."

"I noticed something that made me suspect that crimes worse than murder might be planned. And several other men, it appears, have been killed."

She nodded. "Well, unfortunately I have no murdered people to show you today," she said. "So why are you here?"

"I believe these men were killed because they had parts of a map tattooed on their backs."

"How amusing," she said in a high-pitched voice. "But what does that have to do with me?"

"I have concluded that you had the men tattooed," the judge said. "And that now you have sent someone to take the maps."

Lady Osuni snapped open a folding fan and put it in front of her face, to hide a smile. It was a modest gesture, but she didn't hide her eyes, which showed her amusement as plainly as her mouth would have.

"Believe what you please," she said. "It is of no concern to me."

The judge nodded. "Yes," he agreed. "I have no proof. But I have two of the men in a safe place. So you cannot get the maps on their backs."

"Is that so?" she said, sounding unconvinced.

"However," the judge continued, "you have a map that I cannot obtain. One that comes from the back of a man named Boko."

Lady Osuni merely sniffed at this, as if a bad odor had entered the room.

"You say these two men with maps are safe?" she asked.

"Very safe," the judge responded.

"You see my fish here?" she asked, waving her fan over the pool. "*They* think they are safe. I come and feed them. I even pet them. Did you know that fish like to be petted? Mine are pampered, really. I spoil them. But once a week, I will eat one. Their flesh is very rich because they are so well fed. But safe?" She smiled. "Not from me."

This time she did not use the fan to hide her smile. In the old-fashioned style, she had used gallnut paste to blacken her teeth. The smile was dark, and, it seemed to Seikei, deadly. Suddenly he wanted to go home to check on Bunzo and the two men he was guarding.

"I ask you to give me the map that you took from Boko's back," said the judge.

"I call this one Boko," she replied, pointing to one of the fish. "I'll send you his bones when I eat him."

"I can have your residence searched," the judge said.

Lady Osuni sniffed. "I am the widow—and the mother— of a daimyo," she said. "You will need the shogun's permission to search my house. I think you will find he does not like to annoy me too much."

"Is your son, the current Lord Osuni, at home? I would like to have a few words with him as well."

Seikei thought he saw Lady Osuni's eyes waver, just for

a moment. "He is not at home, and he would answer you in the same way I do."

"One can always hope not," murmured the judge.

"Have you finished?" asked Lady Osuni. "I'm very busy."

"Thank you for your cooperation," said the judge as he got to his feet.

The servant appeared to show them through the house again. Seikei couldn't help scanning the walls as they went, even more closely than on the first time through. He had always enjoyed looking at the calligraphy of the great masters. It was part of a samurai's training to learn to make his own handwriting express emotion, and Seikei was reasonably good at it. But these were wonderful examples.

That was why one stood out from the others as Seikei passed it. For it was not only unlike the work of a master, but remarkably sloppy. He started to draw the judge's attention to it, but realized both he and the servant were several steps ahead. Seikei had to hurry to catch up.

After they left, Seikei wanted to ask if the judge would now ask the shogun's permission to search Lady Osuni's mansion. Before he could, the judge began to speak, half to himself, half for Seikei's benefit: "Lady Osuni's son, though he has inherited the title, is rumored not to be in possession of all his wits. That makes his mother's ambitions all the more puzzling, except of course that a powerful daimyo—no matter how incompetent—can surround himself with wise advisers. Even his mother."

He looked at Seikei. "What kind of business would this young lord be allowed to conduct without his mother's supervision?"

"I can't think of any," Seikei replied.

"Nor can I," said the judge. "So it must be pleasure that has drawn him out of the house. I wonder if the young lord likes to gamble."

16 —
A GAME OF CARDS

Seikei and the judge crossed the bridge into Edo's pleasure quarter, Yoshiwara. It was called the floating world, not only because it was built on what was once a swamp, but because the cares of everyday life drifted away here.

Seeing that it was impossible to suppress the various pleasures that people liked to indulge in, an earlier shogun had set aside this area for them to enjoy themselves. It was sometimes said that there were no rules in Yoshiwara, but that wasn't true. Seikei had worked in a teahouse here to help the judge find out who was setting fires in Edo. He knew that Yoshiwara had its own rules.

Seikei felt more secure now about the two men in the cellar of the judge's house. After leaving Lady Osuni's, the judge had gathered a squad of firefighters and stationed them around his house. Three men were even on the roof, ready with buckets of water. The ninja would have trouble if he tried to set another fire to drive out his quarry.

Bunzo and a dozen other samurai would keep him from entering the house. The guards were impressive, and Seikei felt a tiny bit disloyal to be wondering if the ninja could somehow overcome them anyway.

He and the judge were dressed in plain brown kimonos. Like all samurai, they were required to leave their swords at the entrance to the pleasure quarter. There might be fights in Yoshiwara, but they were seldom deadly.

Virtually every building here was devoted to pleasure of some kind. Pretty women stood in front of most doors, urging people to come inside. Some were *kabuki* theaters. Others were teahouses, where talented geishas offered music, dance and witty conversation along with the tea (or sake, if that was your preference). Still other places specialized in gambling and games of chance. There were too many of these to search each one, so Seikei wanted to see how the judge would choose which to enter.

They walked slowly, listening to the music that drifted faintly from some of the houses. It was still early, so there were as yet no stumbling men who had drunk too much. Seikei knew that despite Yoshiwara's festive appearance, it was really a sad place. Most of the women who worked here had been sold by poor families who couldn't afford to support all their children.

The judge stopped in front of one of the establishments where a banner proclaimed TEST YOUR SKILL.

"What is different about this place?" the judge asked Seikei.

It didn't take long for Seikei to answer. "The man standing at the front door doesn't look as if he wants anyone to enter." The burly man, his arms folded, shot them an unfriendly look.

"Yes," said the judge. "Very interesting. I think we should investigate."

As the judge stepped onto the porch, the man moved to block his way. "Private party," he muttered.

"I am one of the shogun's officials," the judge replied. "I am here to inspect this establishment. Anyone who interferes with my duties is subject to arrest."

The man frowned. Seikei admired the way the judge could change his voice to make people do exactly what he wanted. He stepped past the man, motioning for Seikei to follow. The man did not resist.

Inside, a sickly sweet odor filled the room. Four men were seated around a low table, playing cards. Two of them looked up, seeming surprised to see newcomers enter. They made no objection, however. Off to one side, two older men were playing a game of *go*. Both of them were smoking pipes. Seikei realized they were the source of the sweet smell.

The judge took a seat on a mat next to the card game. Seikei squatted behind him and looked over his shoulder. Three of the men at the table had the distinctive haircuts of samurai. Though they wore no swords, their arrogant expressions also marked them as being among the elite citizens of Edo.

One of them seemed to be the leader, even though he spoke slowly, as if it were difficult for him to think up words. His nose was so flat Seikei thought he must have fallen on it when he was a baby. Yet when he said something intended to be amusing, his companions laughed. Seikei noticed that although most visitors to Yoshiwara donned plain clothing to hide their identities, this man flaunted his. He wore a silken kimono with embroidered irises. Almost certainly, he was Lord Osuni.

The fourth man, who was gathering cards for a new game, was wiry and wore a stone-colored kimono with a pattern of white squares. He glanced at the judge and said, "Two *ban*." The judge nodded, took two coins from a pouch and placed them on the table. Seikei saw that all the other players sat behind stacks of coins.

The dealer spread the cards facedown on the table, making a fan. When his hands were flat on the surface for a moment, Seikei saw the tattooed symbols between his fingers: ya-ku-za. One was partially hidden by a ring, but this was clearly the man they were looking for. Seikei tried not to show his excitement, but the dealer wasn't looking at him. He was staring across the table at one of the three samurai, the one who seemed most important.

The dealer deftly flipped the fan of cards over, showing their faces. Each carried a number from one to ten. As Seikei remembered the game, there were fifty cards in all, five of each number.

The dealer picked the cards up and began to shuffle

them. Each of the three men placed two coins on the table. The dealer flicked a single card facedown in front of each player, as well as himself.

The players looked at their cards. Seikei peeked over the judge's shoulder, trying to see his. But the judge kept it well hidden.

Seikei looked at the other three players. Their expressions varied. One had frowned after looking at his card; a second man smiled slightly. But Seikei recalled that his brother's card-playing friends often deliberately put deceptive expressions on their faces.

The dealer's face, not surprisingly, was blank. Just his eyes moved, flitting from one of his opponent's faces to another.

Only the samurai who seemed to be the leader of the group showed real emotion after looking at his card. He looked quite satisfied with his new possession, like a pampered child. Clearly he was a person accustomed to getting his own way, and fully expected to now. Seikei glanced at the pile of coins in front of him. It was larger than anyone else's. Obviously, the evening had been a good one for him.

The dealer slid two more ban into the center of the table. The other players did likewise—their fee for seeing a second card.

Once again, he dealt each player a card, facedown like the first one. All the men glanced at what they had. The dealer again started the betting—this time with a *koban,* a

larger coin than the ordinary ban. The man on his right shrugged and pushed his cards forward, indicating they weren't worth a bet. The dealer nodded and looked at the next man, the arrogant one. He slowly counted out a stack of coins, pushed them to the center of the table and announced, "Ten kobans." That was too much for the next player, who signaled his surrender.

All eyes went to the judge. To Seikei's astonishment, he matched the ten-koban bet. Seikei had often heard him condemn gambling, saying that the only people who could afford to lose money in such a fashion were the rich. "And if they are that rich," the judge continued, "they should share some with the poor."

"People gamble because they want to win," Seikei had timidly suggested.

"The gamblers who provide places to play and who supervise the games—why do they do that?" responded the judge.

"Why . . . I guess they want to win too," said Seikei.

"And who knows how to play better? Those who make it their occupation? Or those foolish people who come with full pockets thinking they will enrich themselves at a gambling table?"

Seikei saw the point. Yet now the judge was risking— betting!—ten kobans, a considerable sum, on a hand of cards.

The dealer, who had shown no emotion before this, wagged his eyebrows as if he too were surprised. But he

followed that up by putting his own coins on the table, matching the samurai's bet.

The three players who had stayed in the game now turned their cards faceup. In the last round they could ask for as many more cards as they liked, but there would be no more betting.

The samurai showed a four and a six. That was a good hand, Seikei recalled, for only a ten would make him a loser. The judge's cards were both sevens, making his bet all the more baffling. He already had a total of fourteen, so half of all the cards in the deck would put him over nineteen, a losing hand.

The dealer had an eight and a nine. His total of seventeen would be good enough to win most games, particularly since he had the advantage of drawing last. If the other two players went over nineteen, the dealer would automatically win. And if they beat seventeen, he could always draw another card.

The arrogant samurai signaled that he wanted a third card. The dealer turned up an eight. Delight spread over the samurai's face. He could barely restrain himself. With a total of eighteen, he could be defeated only by a nineteen. The dealer would be forced to draw a card, and would almost certainly lose.

First, however, the judge had to play his hand. He indicated he wanted a card, and Seikei held his breath as the dealer flipped one over. Amazingly, it was a four. The judge now also had a total of eighteen. The samurai looked re-

sentfully at him, for it appeared they would have to split the pot—unless, of course, the dealer drew another card and it was a one or two.

The dealer seemed to be preparing to do just that when the judge tapped his finger on the table. "Another card," he said.

Everyone gawked at him. Even the dealer's face changed expression—to one of alarm. "You have eighteen," he pointed out unnecessarily. "Any card but a one, and you will lose."

"Another card, please," the judge repeated.

The dealer drew the deck of cards closer to his body, as if to protect them.

With a movement so swift Seikei would have missed it if he'd blinked, the judge reached out and caught the dealer's arm. He forced it onto the table, carrying the deck of cards with it.

"Another card," the judge said yet again, in his most forceful voice. "Off the top of the deck this time."

The dealer looked at him with a new expression, one of sheer hatred. When he did not move, the judge used his other hand to turn over the card on top of the deck.

It was a one.

17 —
CAPTURED

What's going on here?" the arrogant samurai wanted to know.

The judge pried the deck of cards from the dealer's hand to reveal that the underside of his ring had a shiny piece of metal on it. "This man has been dealing cards off the bottom of the deck," the judge said. "He could tell what each was by looking at this mirror. When he shuffled, he made sure to leave a one on the top, in case he should need it. In fact, he may even have another one there." The judge turned over the next card—also a one.

"So he's a cheat," said the arrogant samurai. "But I've been winning."

"Up till now," said the judge. "I think you were about to hit a losing streak."

The samurai looked at his two companions. "Well, now

that you've exposed him, we'll just take him back to Edo where he can be punished."

"No need," said the judge. "I will take him into custody myself."

"You? What gives you that right?"

"I am Judge Ooka, the shogun's official, acting in his name."

The dealer looked at him with horror and tried to pull away.

The samurai seemed almost as upset as the dealer. "You can't—" he started to say, but then realized he couldn't tell one of the shogun's officials what not to do.

A crafty look came over him. Seikei felt sorry for the man because it was so easy to see what he was thinking. "How do I know you're Judge Ooka?" he said. "Your clothing does not bear the shogun's crest."

"That's right," the dealer piped up. "He could be an imposter. I don't know how that card got onto the top of the deck. Maybe *he's* the cheat and put it there."

The samurai looked uncertain. It seemed to be his natural expression. He glanced at his friends, as if searching for advice. "There's three of us," one said, "and only two of them."

The judge looked at the dealer. "You think you'd be better off with this man, Gaho?" he asked.

"How did you know—" the dealer began before he remembered: "My name's not Gaho."

"I'll make another wager with you, Gaho," the judge continued. "I'll bet you don't know this man's name." He nodded in the direction of the arrogant samurai.

Gaho peered at the man. "I *don't* know his name," he admitted. "I don't need to. When people come to Yoshiwara for pleasure, they leave their names along with their swords at the gate, if they choose."

"But you should," said the judge. "It's worth more than ten kobans to you, Gaho. It could be worth your life."

Gaho licked his lips. Clearly he didn't know if the judge was crazy or telling the truth. Either way he seemed to be in a tight spot. He kept looking back and forth between the judge and the samurai.

"Let him go," the samurai said. "If he cheated anyone, it was me. I'll take him back."

"This is Lord Osuni," the judge told Gaho. "The young lord. He's come here to bring you back to his mother. She wants to collect something from you. Shall I let him take you?"

With a cry of despair, Gaho wrenched free and started toward the back of the room. The three samurai tried to follow, but the judge moved to block them. "Go after him," he shouted to Seikei. "Bring him to the gate!"

"He can't escape," Seikei heard young Lord Osuni say. "I have a guard at both entrances."

But that didn't stop Gaho. He scurried down a narrow corridor with Seikei close behind. A door at the far end

slid open, and a blast of fresh air rushed in. For an instant Seikei saw Gaho outlined in the doorway, and then he was gone.

When Seikei reached the exit, he nearly tripped over the body of Lord Osuni's guard, who was either unconscious or dead. Since Gaho hadn't had the time to do this, Seikei wondered who had.

The question distracted him only for a moment. Off to his right he could hear Gaho's running footsteps. Seikei took off after him. The alley was filled with wooden crates and bags of garbage. Seikei slipped on a wet spot and fell into something sticky.

He got to his feet, breathing hard, and heard the sounds of a scuffle. Someone grunted as if being struck. He ran forward and then tripped over a cord strung across the alley. As he tried to get up this time, he felt someone wrap the cord around his ankles.

Seikei kicked wildly at whoever it was, but missed. A second person grabbed his arms. Seikei cried out, and received a punch in the face that stunned him.

When he recovered, he found himself tied hand and foot and lying facedown in the filthy alley. He heard two people whispering to each other, but the only words he could make out were, "What should we do with this one?" Unfortunately, he couldn't catch the answer.

Then Seikei had that strange feeling again, the one that by now was becoming more familiar. He sensed, rather

than heard, the arrival of another person on the scene. The man pulled Seikei up by the hair, and once more the two yellow eyes peered into Seikei's face.

"Ah," said Kitsune. "The slow learner. You're always too late, aren't you? And too weak."

"My father—" Seikei started to say, but then stopped. Why warn Kitsune?

"Yes, he and Lord Osuni are having a discussion," said Kitsune. "All to the good, for my purposes." He dropped Seikei and said to the other two men, "Bring him along too. And be quick about it. His father will soon want to know where he's gone."

The other men, both of whom were dressed entirely in black outfits that made them nearly invisible in the dark, picked up Seikei and Gaho the gambler, who was unconscious. Just as well for him, Seikei thought. For in a little while Kitsune would no doubt strip his back of its treasure.

Yoshiwara had originally been a swampy wasteland that now was home to shame and secrets and dreams. Kitsune and his men knew all the furtive back alleys where shadows sheltered them from the eyes of the night patrols. When they emerged from the maze of narrow pathways, they came to the edge of the shallow waters that surrounded the pleasure quarter.

Seikei felt himself dumped rudely into the bottom of a shallow boat. Almost at once, the craft was pushed away from the shore. Seikei knew that it was useless to cry out; it

would only earn him a kick in the ribs. Besides, who would notice one more shout in the place where dozens of drunken samurai wandered nightly?

Gaho lay next to Seikei, still breathing, but not able to speak. Seikei knew what Kitsune intended to do with the gambler, but what did he want with Seikei?

Whatever it was, it couldn't be good.

18 —
LADY OSUNI'S COMMAND

*T*he night had been a long one, particularly since Seikei had to spend it with his face against the bottom of the boat. At some point he had felt the craft catch a current, which gradually grew stronger. He guessed they must have reached the Kanda River, which meandered through the city until it reached the Arakawa, a larger stream that flowed into Edo Bay. Did Kitsune intend to take them that far? Or was some hiding place within the city their destination?

Seikei's only hope was that a passing squad of night watchmen would see the boat and investigate.

But no such luck. Occasionally Seikei could hear a far-off bell announcing the passage of the night hours, but aside from that the only sound was the lapping of water against the sides of the boat.

At some point, Gaho began to regain consciousness. He groaned softly at first, and then, when he discovered that

his hands and feet were bound, began to cry out. There was a dull thud, and the noises stopped.

Seikei struggled silently with his bonds, but to no avail. Kitsune's men were too careful to do a sloppy job of tying their captives.

Finally the boat scraped against a sandy bottom, and two of the men jumped out to pull it on shore. By now the sky was becoming pink in the east. It was light enough for Seikei to see, when he was lifted out of the boat and set on his feet.

They were on a deserted section of the waterfront. A larger boat, with a furled sail, was tied up to a rotting dock. Standing at the end of the dock was a slender figure dressed in a dark silk kimono. As Kitsune stepped ashore, the figure came forward and Seikei saw who it was.

Lady Osuni.

"Where is my son?" she said in a cold voice.

"He became involved in a dispute with Judge Ooka," Kitsune replied. "It was impossible to bring him with us."

"That is unacceptable," replied Lady Osuni. "We can't go to Yamaguchi without him."

"I have something almost as good," said Kitsune. He nudged Seikei with his foot. "This is Judge Ooka's son."

Lady Osuni peered at Seikei as if he were one of her koi fish who had mysteriously floated to the surface. "I recognize you," she said. "Do you have any brothers?"

Seikei didn't quite understand. Was she asking about Denzaburo, the younger brother from his original family?

Kitsune knew what she meant, however. "He is the judge's only child, as dear to him as your son is to you."

"Well then, we will allow him to live a little longer," Lady Osuni said. She looked at Seikei and added, "Be careful you do not annoy me."

She then gestured toward the other body lying on the dock. "Which one is this?" she asked.

"Gaho," Kitsune replied.

"Why bring me his body when all we need is the map from his back?"

"When we acquired the other maps," Kitsune said, "there was a tanner available to preserve and mount them. Unfortunately we have had to make our departure from Edo more quickly than originally planned. So the only way to preserve Gaho's map is to let him carry it."

"I am displeased," said Lady Osuni. "This is not what I paid you to do."

"It is my understanding that what you want to do is find the way to the place where . . . certain things are hidden."

"Just so," she replied. "But even *that* seems beyond your capability."

Seikei felt the cold anger that radiated from Kitsune. It was risky of Lady Osuni to question the ninja's competence so openly.

"Including this one," Lady Osuni said, gesturing at Gaho as if he were a thing, not a man, "how many maps have you collected?"

"With the one you had mounted earlier," said Kitsune, "we have five."

"And the other two?"

Kitsune hesitated. "The men I assigned to recover them have not returned."

Seikei hid a smile. Bunzo had been able to protect Rofu and Michio after all.

Lady Osuni turned her back. It was unmistakably a gesture of contempt. Seikei wondered how long Kitsune would take being treated like a servant—a none-too-bright servant.

After a moment's thought, however, Lady Osuni seemed to come to a decision. She faced Kitsune again. "Judge Ooka has those two men in custody, doesn't he?"

"I am certain of it."

"Then kill him."

Even Kitsune was taken aback. "The judge is one of the shogun's closest advisers," he protested.

"What of it?" Lady Osuni snapped. "Once we recover what these maps lead to, I . . . that is, my son, will be as powerful as the shogun."

Seikei thought he saw a flicker of doubt cross Kitsune's face, as if he was realizing just how reckless his employer was.

"In any case, I will pay you well enough," Lady Osuni went on. "After you kill the judge, you can return to that mountain of yours and let me worry about the shogun."

"I cannot—"

"You certainly can. This judge walks about the city with no one to guard him. He even came to my mansion the other day to warn me. Me!" She laughed, a sound that was worse than her anger. "I should have had him killed then."

"Even if I could kill him . . ." began Kitsune.

"Of course you could," Lady Osuni said. "You wouldn't even need to get close to him. He's fat and slow. Use one of those sharp little discs you throw at people. Slash his throat with it. It's a big enough target."

"But his aides will still have the two men with the maps."

"With the judge dead, they won't have any further reason to protect them," said Lady Osuni.

"I see your point," said Kitsune. He glanced at Seikei, who felt uncomfortably as if he were about to be sacrificed. That was all right, he thought, if he could give up his life to save the judge, but he didn't see how that was possible.

All at once, however, Seikei found himself speaking, as if Kitsune had planted thoughts in his head. "You don't need the two men," Seikei announced. "I have made copies of the maps. I'll make some for you."

Lady Osuni looked at him with skepticism. "Why would you do that?" she asked.

"So you won't kill my father," Seikei replied.

"Ha! Save us all that trouble, would you? How do I know you'll make the maps correctly? Or that you're even capable of it?"

In truth, Seikei was a little worried about that too. "I can do it," he said, trying to sound confident. "The judge trusted me to do it properly."

"It would be best if we began our journey at once," Kitsune added. "By now the shogun's guards will have discovered that you've left your residence. They will be searching for you."

"What about my son? Do you propose just abandoning him?"

"Strangely enough, you're fortunate that he fell into Judge Ooka's hands. It's well known that the judge will not torture anyone. In time, he will trade your son for his."

Lady Osuni laughed again. Seikei wished she were not standing so close to him. She turned to him and said, "Always remember that I have no such qualms."

Seikei did not doubt her.

19 —
AT SEA

As the sun's rays shone across the water, the crew raised the sail and untied the lines that held the boat to the dock. Seikei, now released from his bonds, was ordered to go below decks. Probably Kitsune feared that if they passed a shogunate patrol vessel, Seikei might call for help.

In a short time, Gaho the gambler joined him, stumbling down the short flight of stairs that led to the cabin. Gaho looked terrible. Besides showing the effects of being dragged through a filthy alley, the bottom of a leaky boat and a sandy beach, he now appeared to have acquired green skin.

"I'm going to die," he said in the miserable tone of a man who knows no one will care.

"You're probably just seasick," said Seikei.

"Just? I would rather die of something less painful," said Gaho.

"You'll feel better after you throw up," Seikei said, re-

membering his own first sea voyage, with Captain Thunder's gang.

As if motivated by Seikei's suggestion, Gaho promptly did just that. In the nick of time, he managed to grab a bucket that looked as if it were ordinarily used to hold fish. As a matter of fact, when Seikei looked inside, he saw some of Lady Osuni's prize koi. "Better hide that," he told Gaho, who paid no attention.

The gambler stretched out on a straw mat and closed his eyes. "I feel better, but I'm still going to die," he said.

"Why?"

"Because I have something Lady Osuni wants, believe it or not."

"The map?"

Gaho was surprised enough to sit up and stare. "How did you know? Say, you look familiar. Weren't you with that fat old fool who broke up my card game?"

"That was my father, Judge Ooka, the wisest man in Japan," said Seikei. "And if he was such a fool, how was he able to catch you cheating?"

Gaho sighed. "I got too greedy. The three samurai who arrived first clearly were inexperienced and overconfident. I probably could have played honestly and won against them. That tall one—I could see by his face what kind of cards he'd been dealt, even if . . . you know."

"Even if you hadn't seen them with your mirror ring?"

Gaho pursed his lips. "Never hurts to have a little extra help. Anyway, I should have told that fat—I mean, your

esteemed father—that there was no room for more players. But as I say, I thought I could reel in two big fish at the same time."

They heard footsteps and saw Kitsune come down from the deck. "I'm going to show you what you have to work with," he told Seikei. He unlocked a wooden chest and brought out a framed calligraphed poem. Seikei recognized it as being from Lady Osuni's house. It was the poem that had seemed out of place because its quality was so inferior.

Kitsune showed what he thought of it by ripping it out of its frame and tossing it aside. Underneath the poem was a light brown piece of what looked like leather. When Seikei looked a little closer, he saw the now-familiar features of a map inscribed on it. His stomach turned over as he realized it was the tanned and preserved skin from a man's back.

"Boko's map?" he asked, hating the fact that his voice shook.

"This is Boko's," Kitsune confirmed. He brought out other, newer-looking pieces of leather from the chest. "Tatsuo's, Ito's and Korin's," he announced. "That makes four. You have made copies of Rofu's and Michio's. And the seventh . . ." He turned to look at Gaho, who seemed to be trying to sink into the floor.

"I don't know what you're talking about," said Gaho with a squeak. "I never heard of any of those people."

"They were your friends, Gaho," said Kitsune. "You all made an agreement with Lady Osuni."

Gaho hung his head. "It seemed like a good bet," he said. "This crazy woman and her map, which she was never going to need anyway . . ."

"She needs it now, Gaho," said Kitsune.

"I didn't think you could find me," Gaho muttered. "After I heard what happened to Boko, I changed my name. I went from place to place, using a different name each time."

"Every place you went, someone saw you," said Kitsune. "You were never far from Lady Osuni's hands."

Gaho slumped, looking as if he had lost his last koban.

"Your path was the same as those your friends followed, Gaho," said Kitsune. "It always led to death. I would have finished you off long before this, except for Lady Osuni."

"She has decided to be merciful to me?" A ray of hope lit up Gaho's face. The judge had told Seikei that gamblers always think their luck will change, no matter how much they lose.

"No," replied Kitsune. "She wanted her son to have the honor of capturing you. If *honor* is the right word. So he was sent to play cards with you while I waited outside. All he had to do was get you out of there. We were going to take you to a tanner. Of course he couldn't carry out that simple a task, and to keep you out of the judge's hands, I had to step in and bring you here."

Gaho smiled weakly. "So I was lucky last night after all."

"Only until we reach a town with a tanner," said Kitsune. He turned to Seikei. "In the meantime, you get started making copies of the two maps we don't have. Figure out where they fit in with the other five."

"There are only four here," Seikei pointed out.

"Oh, yes," Kitsune said. "I almost forgot." Something shiny flashed in his hand and he sliced down the back of Gaho's kimono.

Gaho screamed, thinking that Kitsune had cut him, but then realized he wasn't feeling any pain. The only thing that had happened was that Gaho's kimono now hung in two pieces, and his tattoo was there for all to see.

"Get to work," Kitsune repeated. "And if this worthless slug gives you any trouble, let me know." He went back on deck.

"He didn't need to do that," said Gaho, picking at the torn cloth. "This is my lucky kimono."

"Lucky for you he missed your back," said Seikei. He put the four maps in front of him. His stomach still turned as he looked at the three that he had first seen on living men. Poor Ito, whose only friend was a monkey. And Korin, who had let his fear take him right into Kitsune's hands . . .

"I can't do this," Seikei said.

"What?" asked Gaho. Seikei was annoyed. He'd been talking to himself, not Gaho.

"Help Lady Osuni overthrow the shogun," Seikei replied.

"Is that what she's trying to do?" said Gaho. "That explains everything. And it's all the more reason why you should help her."

"No," said Seikei. "She's evil."

"She won't hesitate to kill you if you don't help her," said Gaho. "The best you could hope for is that she does it as painlessly as possible. And she isn't that sort of person."

"I am a samurai," said Seikei.

"So was Ieyasu," Gaho replied.

Seikei was puzzled. "What does that have to do with me?"

"Well, he was the first of the Tokugawa shoguns, as you know. Today there are temples and memorial stones all over Japan in his honor. It's almost like he was a kami."

"He was a great man."

"Certainly. Everyone knows that. And do you know how many people he killed?"

Seikei hesitated.

"Of course you don't," said Gaho. "Nobody does. You couldn't count them all. You see, my young friend, people like you and me are like leaves floating on a river. No matter how many of us there are, it's the river that takes us where it wants to go. The river is people like Ieyasu and Lady Osuni. If she succeeds in overthrowing the shogun, then people will build temples to her."

"No," Seikei said. "She won't succeed."

"She might. You and I have nothing to say about it."

"You're wrong. She wants me to make copies of the two

maps she doesn't have. You say I'm only a leaf, but I don't have to do that."

"That's right. You can go up on deck and throw yourself over the side of the ship. I'll go with you. With luck, we'll swim to shore. Can you swim? I can't."

Seikei was angry, but he didn't know if he was angry at Gaho or himself.

"Anyway, if you don't make the maps," Gaho went on, "Kitsune will just go back, kill your father and take the original maps. So you'll die needlessly."

"But with honor," Seikei said. Still, he wondered if what Gaho was saying was true.

"If you stay alive, on the other hand, who knows what will happen?" said Gaho. "I've learned you can't win unless you stay in the game."

"Why are you interested in keeping me alive?" asked Seikei.

"Nobody else on this boat is likely to help me, are they?"

20 —
The Last Link

*Y*ours is the final map," Seikei told Gaho. The ship had been traveling down the coast for two days and nights. While the others slept, Seikei and Gaho were chained so they couldn't escape. Not that there was any place to escape to. Even though Seikei could swim a little, the ship stayed far enough from the shore so that he could never have reached it.

Lady Osuni was impatient for him to complete the work. She seemed to think that threatening to kill Seikei would make him work faster. Actually, it only made him think harder about refusing to do this at all.

Assembling the maps was like doing a puzzle. After Seikei figured out where the two missing maps belonged in the chain, making new copies of them became an easier task. He was pretty sure he'd gotten them right.

Even so, there was no way to be certain. He still didn't understand why there were so many marks alongside the

paths. Soldiers, Rofu had said they were. But no soldiers would still be standing in the same places ten years later.

Discovering that the map on Gaho's back was the last one only raised another puzzle. The path stopped at a place where there was another strange mark: a series of wavy lines. What could that be?

"You know," Gaho said, "now that you mention it, I think the tattooist—what was his name?"

"Tengen," Seikei recalled.

"Yes, that was it. A strange old fellow—all he cared about was tattooing. Well, he said I was the final link in his masterpiece."

"Did he say what the wavy lines meant? Or exactly where this was supposed to be?"

"Not that I recall. We were in Yamaguchi, the castle town of the Osunis. But old Tengen had a paper map he was working from. It could have shown any place in Japan."

"What happened to the paper map?"

Gaho smiled. "That would clear up a lot of things, eh? And if Lady Osuni had it, she wouldn't need you or me. We'd have been fish food long ago."

"My father was told it had to be destroyed so the shogun's officials wouldn't discover it."

"That would make sense. You know, now something else is coming back to me. When Tengen was doing my back, he talked about wanting to see the cave."

"The cave? Is that what the map leads to?"

"I don't know for sure."

"Do you know what happened to Tengen?"

"Never saw him again, but I guess—" Gaho stopped.

"What?"

"Well, Lady Osuni wouldn't want loose ends, would she? If she were going to destroy the map, she wasn't going to leave anyone around who'd seen the full map."

"You mean she killed him."

"The sort of thing she'd do, don't you think?"

Gaho was right, Seikei agreed. And now, as he assembled the parts of the map in the proper order, he realized that *he* would have the full map.

What would Lady Osuni think about that?

He decided to take a little longer before announcing that the task was finished. He needed time—time to enable the judge to find him.

There were a few small portholes in the cabin. Though he couldn't have squeezed through them, Seikei was able to catch a glimpse of the shore from time to time. He wondered if the judge had any idea where Seikei was. By now he must have learned that Lady Osuni had left her mansion and fled the city. That in itself was a crime, but of course the judge knew she had far worse deeds planned.

If the ship was headed for Yamaguchi, where the Osuni castle was, the judge would follow. Seikei was sure of it. But no other ships appeared as the days went by. Most Japanese vessels traveled the Inland Sea, but Lady Osuni's crew followed the outer coast, ordinarily a lonely place. Fishermen

didn't like to venture far out to sea, because of the danger of storms. And if Seikei's rescuers were traveling on horseback, the journey by land would take much longer than the sea route.

Seikei looked at the map he had decided must be first in the series. It was from Korin's back. There was nothing on it that resembled a castle. A large section of the map consisted entirely of wavy lines—and then Seikei remembered that on Korin's actual tattoo, that area was blue. It must be the sea.

If so, then two massive soldiers apparently stood on the very edge of the coast. Between them began the path, marked by the pointing arrows that Seikei had learned looked like a musket.

He had been concentrating so much on the map that he hadn't noticed someone come up behind him. Seikei jumped when he saw a shadow move across the page.

He turned to face Kitsune. The man's unnerving yellow eyes bored into Seikei, who felt they could pierce through any secret.

Kitsune put his finger on the map, between the two soldiers. "Is that where the search begins?" he asked.

"Yes, if there are two soldiers at the right place," said Seikei.

"Lady Osuni assures me they will be there," replied Kitsune. "Have you finished all the maps?"

"Not . . . not completely," said Seikei.

"Lady Osuni is impatient."

"One of the maps was on the back of a firefighter," Seikei explained. "He had burns that made copying the map difficult."

"And him?" Kitsune gestured toward Gaho, who was in a corner trying to make himself invisible. "Are you finished with him?"

"He's actually . . . ah . . . helping me to figure out what the maps looked like originally," said Seikei.

Kitsune gave Seikei a skeptical look, but said only, "We should arrive at our destination by tomorrow. Be ready." He headed back on deck.

"Thank you," said Gaho, in a small voice after the ninja had left.

"It would be lonely if you weren't here," said Seikei.

"You really have finished, haven't you? I saw you place all the maps together."

Seikei shrugged. "I can't be positive I'm right. I won't know until we get there what some of these marks mean."

"Look at it this way," said Gaho. "If you've copied the maps badly, Lady Osuni will have you killed. But if you've done your job right, then you'll no longer be useful and she'll kill you anyway."

"No," said Seikei. "You've forgotten that my father has her son. She won't kill me as long as she wants to get him back."

"The flat-nosed one at the card game?" Gaho recalled. "Was that him?"

"Yes."

"Lady Osuni is going to make *him* the ruler of Japan? Playing cards with him was like toying with a child."

"He didn't seem very bright," Seikei admitted.

"You know what you should do? Convince Lady Osuni that you're her true son, the one who will make her proud and fulfill her ambitions. Let her adopt you, and she can stop worrying about the other one."

"I wouldn't want her to be my mother," Seikei said firmly.

"You shouldn't be so picky," responded Gaho. "She could—"

He was interrupted by Kitsune, who reappeared at the entranceway. "Put the maps away," he told Seikei. "Put them in the waterproof chest. A storm is coming."

21 —
AN ALLIANCE

*T*his time Gaho wasn't the only one who thought he was going to die. Seikei had seen storms on the Inland Sea when he lived in Osaka. But the terrible wind and rain that blew from the Outer Sea was far worse.

Lady Osuni came below too, her face as dark as the sky. She felt personally offended that Susanoo, the kami of storms, had chosen to interfere with her plans. Shouting and shaking her fist, she roamed the cabin, demanding that the storm cease at once.

Gaho had become ill again, and this time of course couldn't use Lady Osuni's fish bucket. So he had tried to go up on deck, and the boat lurched just as he reached the top of the steps. He fell backward, giving his head a nasty crack. Lady Osuni, not surprisingly, was unsympathetic, giving him a sharp kick and a tongue-lashing.

Now Gaho sat in a corner, clutching a bucket of sand that was intended for fighting fires. Gaho was using it for

a different purpose, half-burying his face in it whenever he got sick.

The storm had been raging for hours, but showed no sign of letting up. In Seikei's opinion the crew should have tried to take the boat ashore before the wind reached dangerous levels. Lady Osuni apparently felt they were safer from pursuers if they stayed on the sea. Now, however, it looked as if they would soon be under the sea.

It was frustrating for Seikei to know that his death would have nothing to do with honor or bravery. Susanoo would claim all—the cowardly and the courageous, the good and the evil alike.

The wind howled as if laughing at them, and Lady Osuni screamed back, seeming to think she could out-shout it.

"Stop it!" Seikei yelled at her.

It worked—on Lady Osuni, not the wind. She was so surprised that she shut her mouth, but only for an instant.

Then: "How dare you!" she cried. "I'll have you thrown overboard." Over her shoulder, Seikei could see Gaho silently mouthing pleas for him to stop.

"All your hired men are on deck," said Seikei, "trying to keep the ship afloat. And here you are, shouting at the storm. Who's going to throw me overboard?"

Lady Osuni looked around the room. Perhaps she was trying to find something to kill Seikei with. He didn't care.

He took a step toward her. "All this for your insane quest to overthrow the shogun?"

She looked at him, suddenly wary. "Who told you that?"

The judge did, thought Seikei. Or at least he had figured it out. Maybe he wouldn't want Lady Osuni to learn that he knew it.

Seikei must have glanced at Gaho, because Lady Osuni whirled to look at him. Gaho squeaked and pushed his head deeper into the sand bucket.

She turned back to Seikei. "He doesn't know. None of them knew. You're guessing."

Seikei realized she must think he had learned of her plans from one of the tattooed men. He decided to be mysterious. "I know everything," he told her. He recalled the judge telling him that if a suspect thinks you know what he has done, he will gladly discuss it with you. *"You can learn many things that way,"* the judge had said.

"You do?" said Lady Osuni, but not in a fearful way. She was far more cunning than her son. "What do you know?"

Seikei decided to mention the most important thing that he did know. He was taking a chance, but he was desperate. "I know about the muskets," he said.

He saw that Lady Osuni was impressed. Her nostrils widened and her eyes blazed. She raised clenched fists as if she would like to beat him.

But she thought better of it. "Shosho," she said. "He must have told you. None of *them* knew that," she said, gesturing at Gaho.

Seikei had no idea who Shosho was, but tried to look as

if he did. "I know everything Shosho does—and more," he said.

"Really?" She didn't believe him. "Only *I* know more than Shosho," she said.

"Have you fired a musket?" Seikei asked.

"Don't tell me *you* have," she said. Despite her skepticism, he could see she wanted to believe him. Her eyes glittered.

"I've seen it done at the shogun's castle," he told her.

She nodded eagerly, ready to share her story. "You have? Truly?"

"Yes."

"Then you must know how powerful they are. My husband said that with a hundred of them, he could make himself shogun."

Seikei wasn't so sure of that. "Only a hundred? The shogun has thousands of swordsmen to defend him."

"But don't you see? Their swords are useless against men armed with muskets. Our men will kill their enemies before they even get close."

She put her hand on his arm while describing this. It took great self-control for him not to pull away. What an awful picture of warfare. It was sickening for Seikei to think of men of honor being cut down so easily. But could it really be done?

He thought of the demonstration he had seen at the shogun's palace. All he had seen was the death of a bird,

but the way it fell from the sky . . . so suddenly, as if an invisible arrow had struck it. Seikei shivered.

"Join me," Lady Osuni said.

Seikei felt paralyzed, totally unsure how to respond. He wanted to tell her how loathsome she was, but he knew he must win her confidence in order to stop her.

"You can be of great help," she said. "It won't be forgotten after our victory. And my son . . . Shosho will need advisers."

So *that* was who Shosho was. Well, he would need advisers, that's for sure, thought Seikei.

He noticed Gaho nodding eagerly at him behind Lady Osuni's back. The gambler had no honor, and of course he thought Seikei didn't either. What was the honorable thing to do now? Seikei shook his head to clear it.

"The criminal wants sympathy for what he's done," he suddenly recalled the judge saying. *"To find the truth you must convince him you are on his side."*

And what had Gaho told him? You have to stay in the game if you want to win. There was some truth to that. If Seikei wanted to thwart Lady Osuni's plans, first of all he would have to keep her from killing him. He could at least go along until she ordered him to do something dishonorable.

"I will join you," he said.

The skepticism disappeared from Lady Osuni's face. Seikei realized that he had done exactly what she thought

was the smart thing. Since she had no sense of honor at all, she couldn't understand people who did. She thought any-one should be glad to join her.

"When we reach shore," she said, "you will bring the maps."

"Yes," he said, but the wind still howled outside, as if mocking them. A wave caught the boat and tossed it into the air like a toy. Seikei felt his stomach go with it. Was he doing the right thing? Would he survive long enough to find out?

22 —
CRABS ARE BAD LUCK

When the storm blew itself out at last, Seikei went on deck. What he saw frightened him: nothing but sea in all directions. It was as if the land had simply disappeared during the storm. Sailing in the middle of an empty sea made him feel more lost than he had ever been in his life. He wondered how they could possibly find their way back.

But then, as the sun gradually emerged from behind the clouds, the crew raised the sail and Seikei understood. The sun always rose in the east. From that you could figure out the other directions. If they sailed north long enough, they would reach the coast of Japan.

Unless . . . they had traveled so far to the west that they were beyond the end of Japan. What then? The smugglers he had met in Osaka told him that if you went far enough west, you would reach China, but they were great liars. Under the law of the shogunate anyone who left Japan for

another country was forbidden ever to return. Seikei had heard tales of fishermen who disappeared that way.

Lady Osuni was almost as angry as she had been during the storm. She blamed the crew for allowing the ship to be blown off course.

They were either used to her, or paid so well that they didn't care, and went to work. Lady Osuni then cast a few hints that Kitsune wasn't doing his job either.

The ninja wasn't going to tolerate it. "It was not my choice to make this voyage by sea," he said. "There was time to wait and collect all the information we needed before leaving Edo. Then we could have taken the Tokaido Road. But when you left your residence—"

"If your men were competent, we would *have* all the maps," Lady Osuni snapped back. She must be paying Kitsune *very* well, Seikei thought. He could see the ninja struggling to control his temper.

"Fortunately," Lady Osuni continued, "I have persuaded Seikei here to give me his full cooperation. He is a bright young man, in many ways like my son."

Kitsune's eyebrows rose. "Is that so?" he said in a voice that sounded like fingernails scratching silk. "You're cooperating voluntarily, are you?" he asked Seikei.

"Yes," Seikei responded. He tried to sound loyal and enthusiastic, but it was a struggle.

"How convenient," Kitsune commented, letting Seikei know that at least one person on the ship still did not trust him.

A favorable wind sent the ship northward, and in a few hours land again came into view. Of course, it was unfamiliar because they had no idea what part of the coast they were near.

The land was not directly north of them, and they had to set a northeasterly course. "We've overshot the channel," the ship's pilot told Kitsune. "We have to go back."

Kitsune's face told what he thought of the delay, but there was nothing to do but wait. Finally, in the middle of the afternoon, they reached a wide channel where they turned north. Almost at once Seikei felt the air become warmer and more humid. It was the kind of weather Edo only had for a few weeks in summer. Yet this was still early spring.

The heat, uncomfortable to Seikei, only seemed to invigorate Lady Osuni. She set men to fishing and waited eagerly for them to catch something. "The fish here are the best in Japan," she told Seikei. "Nowhere else is there a warm current to make them grow plump and tender."

As soon as the first fish, a large bluefish, was pulled into the boat, Lady Osuni grabbed it. While the fish was still struggling in her hands, she slit its side with a small, gold-handled knife. Stripping the skin, she cut off bites of the flesh and stuffed them into her mouth. When she noticed Seikei watching, she said, "They must be fresh for the taste to be at its best."

As they traveled through the channel, they passed small islands. Seikei could see strange-looking trees growing on

them, and occasionally a flock of brightly colored birds flashed their scarlet and azure wings across the sky.

"These are things that can only live where it's hot like this," Gaho said. "We're getting close to Yamaguchi." He had come up on deck for air after the storm had passed.

"Why is it so warm?" asked Seikei.

"The warm water that flows from deep beneath the sea," replied Gaho. "People say it comes from an underwater volcano."

"How could a volcano erupt under the sea?" asked Seikei. "Wouldn't the water cool it?"

"Water, fire, constantly are at war with each other," said Gaho. "Here, the power of the fire warms the sea. Strange things happen." The gambler was probably just making up a story, but Seikei felt uneasy.

Later, Gaho brought him some of the fish to eat. "What kind is this?" Seikei asked.

"The sailors called it horse mackerel," Gaho replied.

Seikei tried a piece. "It's soft and mushy," he said. "I don't like it."

Gaho shrugged. "You can eat a lot of things when you're hungry."

Seikei realized he had to keep up his strength, so he forced down the rest of the fish. Watching the sailors pull in a net, he saw some crabs struggling in the mesh. He had always enjoyed eating crabs, and was disappointed to see the sailors throw them back. "Why did you do that?" Seikei asked.

"Lady Osuni hates them," one of the men said. "Bad luck, she tells us. She would have us whipped if we kept them."

Seikei shook his head. How could anyone follow such a crazy person? Then he realized that he himself had agreed to do just that.

The channel was filled with jagged shoals just beneath the surface, and so when nightfall came, they had to anchor to avoid running aground. Lady Osuni and Kitsune argued some more over that decision. Seikei could feel the tension rising between them. Each was ready to blame the other for any little mistake.

Seikei dragged a mat on deck because it was too hot in the cabin to sleep. Even up here, the air was steamy. Seikei almost wished it would rain again. Even the water was still, as if something heavy pressed down on it. Every sound was magnified in the darkness. Insects buzzed and whined all around him, and he could hear hollow scraping sounds as something rubbed against the ship's hull. What could that be? Not a fish, certainly. Something much larger, and hard. It bothered him so much that he dreamed of strange, hard-shelled creatures even when he slept. Their claws reached out for him, and he awoke in a sweat.

23 —
THE STONE SOLDIERS

*I*n the morning, the crew raised the sail as soon as there was enough light to steer by. At midday they emerged from the channel. Land appeared on the horizon ahead of them. The sight elated Lady Osuni. "Yamaguchi," she said. "Where the Osunis rule, not the shogun."

The helmsman was now in familiar territory. He steered a course due east along the shoreline, confident he knew where he was going. Seikei brought the first of the maps on deck and studied it.

He drew his finger along the shoreline to the point at the sea's edge where the path began. The two strong marks on either side of the path still puzzled him. Were they sentries, standing side by side?

The helmsman shouted and Seikei looked up. There they were! Not exactly as he had imagined them, but now he understood that part of the map for the first time. The two sentries were pillars. Not carved ones, but natural for-

mations that seemed to have been here for a very long time.

On the plain beyond the coast, Seikei saw, were hundreds more. Jagged rock sentries, some tall, some short. Only if you had a map could you tell which ones marked the invisible path to a hiding place. Otherwise they were just a random collection of ancient stones.

Seikei's eyes went back to the first two, the starting point of the path. Now he could see that a man—a real man, not a stone—stood there as if waiting for them. He looked vaguely familiar, but Seikei could not see him well enough at this distance to identify him.

Lady Osuni, however, had sharp eyes—and of course she had seen him many times. "Shosho," she called across the water. The man, her son, Lord Osuni, heard her and waved.

Hearing someone standing behind him utter a curse, Seikei turned. Kitsune was there, looking angry. "How did that fool get here?" he said in a low voice.

They landed the boat and Lady Osuni was first to disembark. She and her son embraced. They made quite a pair, Seikei thought. Though Shosho was considerably taller than his mother, he acted as docile toward her as one of her pet koi.

Seikei recovered the rest of the maps from the ship's cabin. "Help me carry these," he said to Gaho.

"I'd just as soon stay here," Gaho protested.

"If Lady Osuni thinks you are no longer useful . . ."

Seikei said, drawing his finger across his throat to finish the sentence.

Gaho gathered up the maps.

As they stepped on shore, Kitsune was questioning Shosho. "I find that hard to believe," Kitsune said.

"Are you doubting my son's word?" asked Lady Osuni.

"Let us say I find it odd that he managed to escape from Judge Ooka and arrive here before we did."

"Well, here he is," Lady Osuni said. "Do you think he is a ghost?"

"Just how did you manage to slip out of Judge Ooka's grasp?" Kitsune asked Shosho. "Tell me, please. I enjoy learning from a master."

"They took me to a mansion, not a jail," Shosho replied. The crafty look came over his face again. "But they forgot to lock the door."

"Forgot."

"Yes. So when no one was looking, I just walked out. There was a horse all saddled by the front gate, so I took it."

"A horse. Waiting for you."

"That's right. So I set out for the Tokaido Road because I knew where Mother was going. I moved fast."

"And led Judge Ooka and his men here."

"And led—" Shosho frowned. That hadn't been part of his story.

"*I* don't see anyone following Shosho," said Lady Osuni. "Do you?"

"Trust me," said Kitsune. "They're waiting to see where you'll go next."

"Is this an excuse for you to break our agreement?" Lady Osuni asked.

Kitsune's mouth set in a straight line. "Once I make an agreement," he said, "I keep it."

"Fine. Then get ready, because we're going to follow the path on those maps at once."

"So get ready," Shosho added, with a wave of his hand as if ordering a servant. As Shosho turned away, Seikei saw the look Kitsune gave him. Seikei was glad *he* hadn't been on the receiving end of that look.

Gaho was still unhappy to be going on the search. "This isn't going to turn out well for either of us, you know," he said to Seikei.

"You're the one who said I should tell Lady Osuni I was her true son."

Gaho shook his head. "Who knew you'd actually try it?"

The first map showed them the direction of the path that led away from the beach. Seikei compared it with what he saw on the landscape. There were so many of the tall rocks . . . Then he saw the pattern the mapmaker had intended. "Up there," he pointed, and started to walk.

Lady Osuni left her servants and crew with the boat, taking along only Kitsune and Shosho. "As long as we reach our destination," she said, "we can defeat any number of people who might, or might *not,* be following us."

Seikei realized that Lady Osuni thought the weapons were more powerful than they really were. At least, more powerful than *he* thought they were. He hoped he was right, because if he wasn't . . . He shook his head. He *had* to be right.

The first map was fairly clear, and they soon came to the end of the path marked on it. Seikei was certain he knew which map to switch to now. But it was the one that had been on the back of Michio, the firefighter, and so it was the hardest to read.

"What's wrong?" asked Lady Osuni as Seikei hesitated.

"The marks are hard to read," Seikei explained.

"Well, of course they are," she said. "It wasn't intended that anyone could just walk up to the hiding place. But you have seen the original of this map. It should be easy for you to find the way."

"Maybe he needs some encouragement," said Shosho, touching the hilt of his sword. Seikei regretted, not for the first time, that his own swords had been left behind at the gate to Yoshiwara.

"That way," he said, making his best guess. If the judge and Bunzo really had followed Shosho, maybe the best thing was to keep Lady Osuni wandering aimlessly. Sooner or later the judge would arrive.

Or maybe not. Seikei told himself he couldn't count on being rescued, like a child who's always getting into trouble. He was in a position where he could thwart Lady Osuni's plans. If he pretended not to be able to read the

maps, sooner or later she would just take them away. He should help her find the muskets, and then . . .

And then?

Well, he'd think of *something.* Perhaps Lady Osuni wouldn't know how to operate the muskets. She seemed surprised when Seikei said he did.

"Well?" It was Lady Osuni, wanting to know where they should go next.

"Up there," said Seikei, guessing again.

They reached the top of a hill and saw hundreds more of these tall, jagged rocks ahead. "Coral," Lady Osuni commented when she examined one of the rocks. "This area was once under the sea."

She should feel right at home, Seikei thought.

As they reached the final landmark on the second map, Seikei held his breath. If his guesses had all been correct, then they should be at the beginning of the third map. Gaho handed it to him and he unrolled it. He could feel the others looking over his shoulder as he studied it.

He felt huge relief as he realized that yes, the maps did match up. There, right in front of them, was the first landmark on map three—a trio of coral "soldiers." He stepped forward confidently. The others followed.

24 —
THE END OF THE PATH

*B*y late afternoon, they had reached the end of the fifth map. Seikei had mixed feelings—triumph at having successfully decoded the maps, and fear as the group came ever closer to the hiding place.

"Perhaps we should stop for now."

Everyone looked at the speaker with surprise. It was Kitsune. Seikei thought he looked out of breath, which was impossible, for ninjas pride themselves on their physical endurance.

"What do you mean?" asked Lady Osuni angrily. "We can't stop when we're this close."

"It will be night soon," said Kitsune. "If we haven't reached the end by then . . ."

"We will," said Lady Osuni. "And your hesitation is only slowing us down." She turned to Seikei. "What next?"

Seikei pointed to the next landmark. As he looked around, he saw that they had been continually moving to

lower ground. The rock-filled plain was shaped like a giant bowl. If it had once been under water, as Lady Osuni said, a huge pool must have collected here.

He had been wondering about one of the landmarks on map six. Shaped differently than any of the other marks, it was a circle with ten lines extending outward from the center. Suddenly Seikei saw it—or what must be it—in front of him. He was stunned. It was the shell of a crab, bleached white by the sun. But it was a crab of enormous dimensions. Each of its ten legs was almost as long as a man. He shivered as he imagined what it would have been like alive. It could have crushed a horse in its legs.

"Takaashigani," Lady Osuni growled in a hate-filled voice, as if confronting her worst enemy.

"A giant spider crab," Gaho whispered to Seikei. "Some say that they lived long ago, but there is a story that when Lady Osuni's husband was killed, a crab like this carried off his body."

Seikei remembered that the judge had said the same thing when he was questioning Ito. "That must be why she hates crabs," he said.

With a cry, Lady Osuni stamped on the body of the long-dead creature, breaking a hole in it. "They eat the dead," she said, as if that were enough explanation.

Still kicking the shell, she shifted it a little. "Wait!" said Seikei. "The two front legs are supposed to point to the next landmark. Don't move it!"

"Let's get on with it then," she said. "I despise these foul things."

They moved on, and came to the end of the sixth map without any further incidents. By now the sun had sunk below the rim of the great basin they walked through, and the rocky landmarks cast longer shadows.

"Hurry up!" said Lady Osuni.

Seikei did his best, wondering if there really was a cave at the end of the last path, and how they were going to see inside it, at night. He noticed Kitsune was looking behind them more frequently now. "Stop worrying," Lady Osuni told him. "We're nearly there."

Seikei sneaked a look too, hoping for some sight of the judge and Bunzo. But there was nothing but the darkening sky and the looming stones. They seemed threatening now, as if the soldiers they represented would come to life at night.

Three more landmarks . . . then two . . . and finally they came to a high, wide stone covered with shrubbery. Was this it?

Then Seikei felt water lapping against his sandals and looked down to see a stream trickling away from the rock. He followed Lady Osuni, who was pushing aside some of the bushes that partially concealed the face of the stone.

And there it was. An opening large enough for a person to stoop and crawl through. But beyond was nothing but darkness.

"We can't go in there." It was Kitsune's voice again.

Seikei turned to see what, on anyone else's face, he might have called a look of fear.

"Of course we're going in," responded Lady Osuni. "We didn't come all this way just to gape at a hole in the rock."

"There's no light."

Lady Osuni triumphantly produced a small metal box from a pack. "There's a burning coal in here. We can make torches from these branches."

When Kitsune had no answer for this, Lady Osuni motioned to her son. "Come, Shosho. Help me. And you too," she ordered Seikei and Gaho.

They fell silent while gathering and binding the branches. Then Seikei heard something in the distance. He raised his head. So did everyone else as the sound grew louder.

Hoofbeats, echoing across the rocky plain. No way to tell how far away they were, but clearly there were several riders.

"Ooka," muttered Kitsune. Pointing to Seikei, he told Lady Osuni, "We can use him as a hostage and bargain our way out of here."

"Why should I want to get away when in a short time I will possess the most powerful weapons in Japan?" Lady Osuni said coldly.

"You don't know how many men Ooka has," Kitsune argued.

"Nor do I care. A ninja worried about being outnum-

bered? I see that your reputation was inflated. Stay here then, and surrender. Or come with me and triumph!" She pushed Seikei forward, handing him a flaming torch. "Lead the way."

The only way to stop her, Seikei thought, was to go along and make sure she couldn't use the muskets. If Kitsune refused to enter the cave, then perhaps Gaho would help and they could overpower Shosho.

"I'll go," Kitsune said in a voice that came close to wavering. Seikei recalled what Rofu had said—that Kitsune would lose his powers underground. Could that be true? Was that the reason for his fear?

Pushed from behind, Seikei ducked and edged his way through the hole. He held his torch high as he emerged on the other side—and gasped.

He stood inside a cavern that was so large he couldn't see the top of it. The sound of dripping water echoed from all sides. Bizarrely shaped rock formations threw eerie shadows wherever he pointed his torch.

Gaho was next to come through. "What a hiding place this would make," he said.

"That's just what it is," replied Seikei.

"Have you noticed? It's also much warmer here than it is outside."

Seikei nodded, thinking of the oddly warm channel their ship had passed through earlier.

Shosho came through the hole. He waved his torch around long enough to see how big the cave was. It seemed

to confuse him. He turned to Seikei. "Where are the weapons?" he asked.

Seikei hesitated. He had never seen a cave this large. Even with three torches, there were still dark areas ahead where nothing could be seen.

Kitsune struggled through the hole next. He was breathing hard—very strange, thought Seikei, for it took no great effort to get through the hole. As the ninja took a look at the vast space that surrounded him, his face fell and his knees seemed to wobble.

Lady Osuni finally made her appearance. She turned her head from side to side, her bright eyes shining. She surveyed the scene like an owl preparing to hunt prey.

"Well? Well?" she asked, but no one had anything to say. In typical fashion, she stepped forward, and the others could only follow.

The dripping water, running off the plain above ground, had shaped the walls of the cavern in odd ways. On one side, Seikei saw a series of steps with water flowing down them. He wondered for a moment if they could lead the group to something important.

Lady Osuni ignored them. She moved ahead, waving her torch. "Shosho!" she cried, bringing her son next to her. "Come! Come see the weapons that will make you the shogun!"

Seikei hurried to catch up to them. His feet splashed through puddles. The water here seemed slightly deeper.

Then he heard another sound, quite different from the

dripping and splashing. A scraping sound. Something hard tapped on the stone, then abruptly ceased. Seikei had a feeling there was a living thing not far ahead. Listening.

"Mama?" he heard Shosho say. "I thought I saw something."

"The weapons?"

"No. Something moved."

"It's just a shadow from the torches," Lady Osuni said.

Then Seikei saw it. Or part of it. Just ahead was a crevice on the floor of the cave. Not very wide—they could easily have jumped over it to go farther on. But what looked like one of the pointed rock formations slowly moved up from the depths below.

Only it wasn't a rock. It was like a long seashell. As Seikei stared, it kept getting longer, continuing to rise from the crevice till it nearly reached the ceiling.

"Mama, it's not a shadow," said Shosho. "It's— AAAAAAA!" He let out a terrible scream as the moving thing shot out and snapped shut on his leg. Shosho's torch fell to the watery cave floor, where it hissed and then guttered out. Clumsily he unsheathed his sword and began to hack at the thing that held him.

His mother ran to help, but as she grabbed him around the waist, a second jagged, sharp shell emerged from the crevice and clutched her as well. She tried to push it away with her torch, but the thing was impervious to pain.

Seikei watched in horror as a round hard disc with jagged edges rose slowly from the crevice like an evil sun

bringing dawn. Both of the shell-like claws that held the Osunis were attached to it. They were its legs. But the creature had more than two—they kept popping out of the crevice. Four, then six, then seven, Seikei counted as he dodged out of their way. On top of the central disc were two eyes on stalks, and Seikei felt their terrifying gaze fall on him for a moment.

Fortunately for him the thing was more interested in the prey it had already captured. Both Lady Osuni and her son were screaming so loudly now that Seikei wanted to clap his hands over his ears. More legs encircled the two struggling figures: eight, nine, ten.

The creature, for it was all one huge monstrous being, held them so securely by now that they almost ceased to struggle. It began to pull them inexorably into the crevice. Its hideous head disappeared first, and then, as Lady Osuni and her son cast desperate looks in Seikei's direction, the legs pulled them inside as well.

For a horrible moment, their screams continued, but then died away. Seikei looked around him. Back toward the cave entrance, a single torch still flickered. Was Kitsune there? Or had he abandoned his mistress when she needed him most?

25 —

A Voice in the Darkness

*N*umb and shaking, Seikei walked back toward the remaining torch. As he drew closer, he saw that the person holding it was Gaho the gambler.

"What happened?" Gaho asked. "What was all that screaming? Where are—"

"The weapons had a guard to protect them," Seikei said. "Do you remember the dead crab we saw on the way here?"

"Yes."

"It had a brother. Or maybe a mother. I don't know. It . . ." He couldn't describe it any further. He just gestured toward the darkness behind him, where once again the only sound was dripping water.

"Do you think they're—?" Gaho asked with a look in that direction.

"Yes," said Seikei. "There is no hope for them."

"Odd, isn't it?" said Gaho. "I mean, the way she seemed

to hate crabs so much. Do you think it was the same one who carried off her husband?"

"It may have been," said Seikei. "What happened to Kitsune? I can't believe he ran away."

"No, come see. You can do anything you like to him now."

Kitsune was lying in a watery place. His eyes flickered as Seikei approached, but they were like candles about to reach the end of their wick.

"You've trapped me," he said.

"I?" Seikei was astonished. "I came here against my will."

"You read the maps for Lady Osuni. She would never have found this place on her own."

"She was going to kill me," Seikei reminded him.

"And what happened to her? And that foolish son of hers?"

"Something lives in the cave. An enormous crab. It took them away."

Kitsune laughed and then, because it hurt him, he coughed. "You knew that all along, didn't you?"

Seikei could hardly believe the accusation. "No, I had no idea."

"And you knew, you must have known, what being underground would do to me. Who told you? Rofu? It must have been."

"I first *met* you in a cave," said Seikei. "Don't you remember?"

"That was a shelter on a mountain," Kitsune replied. "This . . . this . . ." His eyes searched the walls of the cave, looking for a way out. "I can feel the ground pressing against me. My kami cannot protect me here."

He looked at Seikei and took a deep breath. Seikei sensed what was coming. But it took a great effort for Kitsune to say it. "Help me. Get me out of here."

Seikei hesitated, torn between pity and fear.

Gaho seemed surprised. "What are you waiting for?" he asked Seikei.

"If I take him aboveground, his power will return," said Seikei.

"So why are you even thinking about it? Kill him."

"But . . . he's helpless."

"Of course he is. Do you think I'd suggest it if he weren't?"

"I can't kill a man who is unable to defend himself."

"If I'm playing cards and I have a winning hand, I raise the bet. I don't worry that it's not fair to those who have a losing hand."

"This isn't a card game," said Seikei.

Gaho shrugged. "If it's not, then I can't help you." He turned and walked off.

"Where are you going?" Seikei asked.

"There's nothing for me here, so I'm going back aboveground. Somewhere I'll find some people who want to test their skill at cards."

"The judge will stop you, if he's there," Seikei warned.

"I'll take my chances on that. I've done nothing wrong."

Seikei didn't reply. He stood there until Gaho's torch was out of sight.

"Are you going to help me?" Kitsune asked.

After a moment, Seikei said, "No."

"Why not?"

"Because you're like Gaho."

Kitsune snorted weakly. "If you're going to let me die, you might at least have the courtesy not to insult me."

"Gaho's a leaf, like he said. He'll go where life takes him. He won't ever change. That's what he will always be. And you . . . are a ninja."

Kitsune seemed to gain strength from this. "There's nothing wrong with being a ninja," he said. "People have always wanted ninjas to perform services for them. I could be of great help to *you*. Those weapons are still here in the cave, aren't they?"

Seikei stepped back, as if Kitsune had suddenly become dangerous again. "I don't want them," he said. "If they're here, I hope they stay buried forever."

"They won't, I assure you. Someone will find them and use them, even if you don't."

"I hope not," Seikei said quietly.

"You were willing enough to help Lady Osuni get them."

"I had to make sure she couldn't use them."

"That's just an excuse," said Kitsune. "You would have served her willingly."

Seikei shook his head. "No. She had never really seen one of these weapons. She had the idea that they were some kind of magic sticks that could be used to defeat any number of warriors. I have actually seen one of them demonstrated. You might kill one person with it, but then it takes time to prepare it to kill someone else. She would have needed many, many thousands of them to overthrow the shogun."

"You don't know how many weapons there are," said Kitsune. "It's a big cave. There *could* be thousands. And if you had them, men would follow you." His voice was like the silken web a spider spins to entrap its prey. "I would help you to gather them. I know many who would join you. Good men, not like Gaho. The crab is nothing. . . . I have poisons we could use on it."

Seikei began to hear Kitsune's words as if they were coming from inside his own head. "You would be the most powerful man in Japan. You could live in the shogun's castle. People would do whatever you wanted them to. Everyone would admire you, even your father. Judge Ooka would—"

Seikei turned and began to walk away. It was difficult, like walking against a strong wind, but he knew he had to do it before he started thinking like Kitsune.

"Stop!" Kitsune called. "If you leave me here, I'll die."

"I'll tell Bunzo where you are. He can decide what to do

about you." Bunzo wouldn't fail this time. Of that Seikei was sure.

Kitsune's voice was fainter now, but Seikei still heard him snarl: "You're a fool."

Seikei nodded. "Yes," he said. "But not a leaf."

AUTHORS' NOTE

Nearly two thousand years ago, Chinese travelers visited Japan and wrote about the practice of tattooing. It never caught on in China, although it was common among Pacific Islanders and Native Americans. Even Egyptian mummies have been found with tattoos.

In Japan, the social acceptability of tattoos changed over time. Some rulers ordered criminals to be tattooed as a means of identifying them. Samurai warriors in pre-Tokugawa times used tattoos to enhance their ferocious looks. Workers who shed most of their clothes on the job often decorated their backs and chests.

Typically the Japanese made tattooing into an art form. Sometimes men decorated their entire bodies, except their faces, with elaborate designs that could take months or years to complete. These were most common in the nineteenth century.

Yes, there really are giant crabs living in Japan to this

day. They are called *takaashigani,* or the Japanese spider crab, and are the world's largest. These creatures, which live as long as a century, may have a leg span as large as seven meters (twenty-two feet). Most of them are found in the waters of the Pacific Ocean off Japan's coast.

The channel through which Lady Osuni's boat traveled is called the Bungo Suido. It is the place where three of Japan's four main islands meet, and is noted for its warm current, which causes unusual plants and sea creatures to grow there.

Yamaguchi province (parts of which were called Suo province in Seikei's time) is at the western end of Japan's largest island, Honshu. Yamaguchi contains an immense system of caves that were named Akiyoshido by Crown Prince Showa (who would become Emperor Hirohito) during his visit in 1926. By some estimates, the caves extend over 420,000 square meters (4.5 million square feet), which would make them the third-largest cave system in the world. Above the caves are the Akiyoshidai plains, which are covered in jagged rocks made of dead coral, formed long ago when the area was under water. Continually dripping water from the plains created the underground caves. Today, tourists can visit some, but not all, of the caves. They are illuminated by electric lights, and so are a little disappointing to some who were expecting a spooky place. The hidden weapons are entirely from our imagination, as is the Osuni family.

Tokugawa Ieyasu did in fact carry a statue of Marishi-ten

with his army, and she looked as we describe her in these pages.

Today, Japanese criminal gangsters are called *yakuza;* the word's original meaning came from the card game, as we describe.

As readers of our previous books know, Judge Ooka was a real person who lived in Japan in the early eighteenth century. He became widely known for his honesty and his clever solutions to crimes, which has caused people to call him the Sherlock Holmes of Japan. The character of Seikei is the authors' creation.